Copyright - C~~...~~ iah **Koh**

Find his wo iahkoh

The right of Bha vork has been asserted in ~~...~~ and 78 of the Copyright, Designs and Patents Act 1988.

All rights reserved. No part of this publication may be reproduced, distributed, or transmitted in any form or by any means, including photocopying, recording, or other electronic or mechanical methods, without the prior written permission of the publisher, except in the case of brief quotations embodied in critical reviews and certain other non-commercial uses permitted by copyright law. For permission requests, write to the author, addressed "Attention: Permissions Coordinator," at the following email address: bhavinp.1994@gmail.com

In this work of fiction, the characters, places and events are either the product of the author's imagination or real but may not be used entirely fictitiously. Any resemblance to actual persons, living or dead, is purely coincidental.

Chapters

Prologue 9

Hero 10

Perfect Beginning 15

Escape 17

One Day 22

Sinaloa Cartel 27

First Date 31

Street Lights 38

Missing 42

Don't Look Down 47

Empire 51

Trap Door 56

I See Fire 60

High Hopes 64

Champion 69

Goodbye, Apathy 72

Crazy Love 79

Madness 84

Strangers 89

Fear 94

Nirvana	101
Runaway	106
Biggest Regret	113
The Hardest Part	118
Grapheos	123
Au Revoir	130
Ordinary Human	135
Run	140
Changes	145
Weakness	150
Wait	158
Come Home	163
In The Middle	168
Turn Around	172
Demons	177
Life in Colour	183
Lost My Way	187
Murder	192
Live Forever	196
Acknowledgments	199

For My Family…

THE FRONT

Prologue

Evolution. Each one of us exists because of the evolution of life that's happened over millions of years on Earth. What makes us special is our consciousness, but that makes us complacent. Humans have reached their potential, they say. Where do we evolve from here? What's *our* next step? Nature can still take its course. Each year new human beings inherit genetic code and mutations in this code cause each individual to be different. For better or for worse. So let's take our next step.

Human beings that are born to develop stronger and smarter.

What if we could gain control? Gain that power?

* * *

Pittsburgh, Pennsylvania. Just east of the Leones household is Kindred Hospital. The whole family is in attendance to see the newest addition to the family, Adrian. Baby Adrian has no way of making sense of the world around him. He has no idea where he is. No sense of how he's able to gaze upon a new world. Yet, he is surrounded by people that seem familiar. His blood relatives; mum & dad, grandma and cousins. The connection of human consciousness is seen by everyone when they are new to the world. They sense nothing else except another human. As people grow, they lose sight of the purity they once saw. The power of the human consciousness will never be realised.

Hero

"Adrian, the bus is here," shouted Mrs Leones up to Adrian's bedroom. Adrian's slim figure emerged, not the tallest but it meant he had better balance and drew less attention to himself. At sixteen years old he was becoming more aware of how he presented himself to his classmates. The clearest sign of this was his short brown hair, made to look ruffled-up but it was evident he had spent some time at the mirror. Unfortunately he was not able to spend as much time on his fashion. Adrian was forced to wear school uniform for the final year; black shoes and trousers with a navy blazer and dark blue tie. Adrian wore his tie loose and high, a small sign of rebellion. A grey Converse shoulder bag completed his outfit, reflecting the style shown by today's youths and highlighting the importance of brands.

Adrian ran down the stairs and made for the door.

"Don't I get a bye?" exclaimed Mrs Leones as she walked into the lounge area.

Adrian sighed and reluctantly replied. "Bye." He grinned at his mum and left the house.

Just like any other morning Adrian climbed onto the bus and sat next to his friend Erik near the back. Erik had been Adrian's friend since they both started junior school together. He was computer smart and always fun to be around. Erik and Adrian, like most friends, had a similar understanding of an unusual situation when it occurred. Such as the time their English teacher Mrs Fletcher and former assistant Mr Mathers would take part in a discreet yet so obvious game of flirtation. Mr Mathers is a former assistant as he could no longer take the inappropriate demands to 'pick up' Mrs Fletcher's various stationary items.

Adrian of course had his own love interest. Sitting three rows from the front was Hannah, a shy but bright brunette. From the moments they have spent alone Adrian could sense their chemistry. He was convinced something was there. Like a candle waiting to be lit.

"Are you going to spend more time with her today?" questioned Erik.

Adrian turned to his friend and looked at him with an uncomfortable expression before dropping his head.

Erik smiled. "For a guy chasing a girl you don't show a lot of confidence." Adrian continued looking down.

"Adrian, its fine! Go and talk to her, I'll help you." continued Erik.

Adrian's expression turned to anger. "I don't need your help! I'm going to talk to her... I like talking to her." He continued to stare at the floor.

"Yeah well, I wish you the best with that." A bemused Erik seemingly accepted Adrian's position as the bus pulled up outside Pittsburgh High School. The school was built to cater for around a thousand students making it one of the largest in Pennsylvania.

Though the window of the bus Adrian could see the path of tarmac leading up to the school's front entrance. *Math, Geography, English and then lunch.* He headed off to his first class of the day. Each department was given its own block. His maths class was down a long corridor left of the entrance, a hallway also leading to the playground and playing field. The entrance to the school led to a spacious open plan reception area. The reception desk was straight ahead next to a couple of cushy red leather sofas surrounding a glass coffee table. Stairs on the right ran up to the first floor where Adrian had his Geography class. To the left was another long corridor connecting the staff room, offices and the English department.

Adrian and Erik were finally reunited in their final class before lunch, English. They sat on a two person table at the front, one row from the door. Through the windows behind them was the small paved area in front of the school's entrance. Erik was quick to try and get the gossip from Adrian's day so far and more importantly the lesson Adrian and Hannah shared.

"So... did you talk to Hannah?" questioned Erik.

"What is it to you?" Adrian was immediately flustered.

Erik rolled his eyes and shrugged. "I'm just curious."

A confident Adrian looked at his friend and threw him a cheeky smile. "You'll have to wait until tomorrow to find out."

Erik instantly looked confused. "What is that supposed to mean?"

THE FRONT

Adrian glanced over to Hannah who was sitting a few rows back. She noticed him and smiled back. Adrian turned back and looked straight ahead as his confident smile continued.

"Just wait."

"Okay, let's get started." Their teacher Mrs Fletcher quickly grabbed the classroom's attention from the front. She started by discussing the difference between an old Fairy advertisement and a modern one. Erik raised his hand.

Mrs Fletcher focused her glare at him. "Yes."

Erik was slightly alarmed by Mrs Fletcher's uncomfortable stare. "Well... miss... One of the adverts is in black & white and the other is in colour." Mrs Fletcher sustained her glare and her expression did not change. But Erik braved more words. "I think I just saved us an hour Miss." Erik scanned the room to see if any of his classmates would laugh along. The room fell silent.

Mrs Fletcher waited a moment before replying. "Erik, this isn't the time. Just listen, this will be useful for your coursework."

Erik nodded, still smiling. However he turned to an unimpressed Adrian and stopped smiling, quietly whispering to himself. "I swear that joke sounded funnier in my head."

Adrian shuddered.

An eerie silence gripped the room.

The door burst open and within seconds a masked figure appeared. The students stopped as they all saw the pistol in the man's left hand. Mrs Fletcher hung onto to the whiteboard pen she was holding as two more covered bodies brushed past her and surrounded the classroom. The gunmen were wearing plain black clothing from their shoes to their leather jackets. The masks were three-hole balaclavas allowing only the eyes and mouth to be seen.

The gunman at the door started to wave his pistol in the direction of the students. "Everybody down on the floor where I can see you. NOW!" The voice sounded masculine and full of authority.

The students lay down, face on the floor. Erik tilted his head to face Adrian, whose expression was full of panic. But although Adrian was frightened he started to think about the positions of the gunmen. One was stood at the door while another was next to Mrs Fletcher near the whiteboard. The third was guarding the windows at the back of the classroom.

"All of you, hands on your head, I don't want to see anyone reaching into their pockets for a mobile!" The voice was now more urgent and serious.

At the corner of his eye Adrian saw Mrs Fletcher stand up. She held her hands behind her head and looked straight at the gunman next to her.

"I don't care what you're here for, I'm protecting these students! You cannot hold a gun to us!"

The second gunman responded, a feminine voice. "Ma'am please get down on the floor or I will shoot!"

Mrs Fletcher resisted the urge to sit back down and continued to negotiate with the woman. "Please! Take what you want and go. You don't need to hurt us!"

The woman was getting impatient. She clicked the back of the gun and pointed it at Mrs Fletcher. The other two gunmen looked anxious, exchanging worrying glances at each other. Mrs Fletcher and the students needed a hero.

"Stop, don't shoot!" A defiant Adrian rose from the depths of the classroom. His voice was loud and sharp.

He took the short walk to the gunman at the door. The third figure at the back of the classroom trained his gun on the intent Adrian. Like a sixth sense Adrian looked back. "Shoot me... I dare you."

Adrian turned back towards the gunman at the door. He punched the gunman's arm, knocking the pistol onto the floor. Before the gunman could react Adrian swung his fist into his face, instantly knocking him unconscious. The gunman at the back had seen enough. He fired a bullet out of his pistol.

Adrian fell to the floor.

The classroom fell silent. Underneath his mask the gunman smiled. But it was too soon. An unharmed Adrian rose to his feet once again holding the dead man's pistol. In a fraction of a second Adrian fired the gun in the direction of the man at the back, piecing his arm. Adrian watched on as the second gunman dropped on the floor.

THE FRONT

Now his attention was focused on the last armed body. The female held her gun up against the side of Mrs Fletcher's head. "You wouldn't, you're just a kid." Her words echoed across the room.

Adrian did not flinch. The woman grew impatient. She moved her gun down and shot Mrs Fletcher in the right leg causing her to fall to the floor in agony.

"That made her get down." The confident women proclaimed.

Anger overcame Adrian. He raised his gun and fired. The women fell straight to the floor onto her back. The sound of her head colliding with the solid floor reverberated into the ears of every student. A puddle of rich red blood filled the area around her.

The classroom fell silent once again.

Adrian ran over to a shaken Mrs Fletcher. The students could finally catch their breath. The tension had subsided.

But the worst was yet to come.

Perfect Beginning

Twelve years ago. Adrian was born into luck. He was already a capable child and he was raised in one of the more loving and financially secure households. His father worked as a finance officer for the American football team Pittsburgh Steelers whilst his mother worked as an estate agent in the local area. The place Adrian called home was a spacious 3 bedroom detached house in the Manchester area. With Adrian being the only child one room was left spare. The colour neutral room consisted of just a bed and a chest of drawers. In the other corners though, lay stacks of used children's toys ranging from small teddy bears to plastic guns. To Adrian, this was his extended play area.

Across the small hallway was Adrian's room. Three walls a neutral white, with one wall holding blue wallpaper with one distinct shape in the centre. Four sharp lines mapped out the shape of a diamond enclosing a coat of pure red paint. Adrian's bed faced this wall; it was something unique that always caught his eye. But it was not the only special feature in his room. Above his head was a predominantly black ceiling with white dots scattered around. Adrian could look up at night and gaze upon the glow in the dark spots and pretend to fall asleep amongst the stars. There was always something bigger where his imagination could take him. The view from each room in the house wasn't luxurious. All they saw were the houses opposite and the roads that separated them.

Adrian learned a lot from his babysitter, Kelly. Kelly had a positive impact on Adrian, mainly due to her ambitious nature. She was a character intent on making the most of her opportunity in the world, unlike many who sacrifice their education for fame and popularity. Even though she was only in the job for a year, Adrian sensed her positivity and later on in life mirrored her hard-working, mature and professional attitude.

Each day he grew stronger, more aware and more conscious.

* * *

THE FRONT

Adrian was raised a free thinker. All the different factors associated to his upbringing were constructive; it meant he knew his right from wrong and more importantly he knew how to think for himself. This helped him develop a unique perspective and the ability to see the bigger picture. His decisions were always based on logic but that did not mean he lacked faith. He trusted his own judgement. Academically Adrian showed a lot of potential but his grades were usually average. An independent thinker, he would often challenge his teachers and stay behind after class to finish his work. He never gave up on a problem easily. The teachers warmed to his enthusiasm. It helped Adrian develop a friendly personality and quickly became a relatable character for everyone in the classroom. When Adrian was on his own his mind would take the high road. He would always ponder the big questions of life, never quite reaching any answers.

Why do we exist? Am I special? Is this world built for me?

Adrian noticed his extra strength as a ten year old. He took the time to understand his strength and his limits. Another sign of his intelligence and awareness. When Adrian was out with his friends he would pick up stones and challenge them to throw them further than him. Adrian's stones got notably further than his friends who decided to take no notice of the competition, not wanting to point out their efforts looking futile in comparison. They would then usually end their days playing baseball at the local field, with Adrian holding back any big swings.

The sun would dip below the trees surrounding the field painting a beautiful scene and highlighting the beauty of the natural landscape. It was the main reason the group returned to the field every evening. Adrian saw it as the perfect end to the day. His friends would rotate positions on the field; batter, pitcher and fielder. Their shouts and laughter would echo across the local community. After an hour or so they would return home. Adrian would be welcomed by his mother, who would already have set the table for their meal.

Life was a present for Adrian. He saw an opportunity to do things right. The world was ahead of him and it looked brighter than ever.

Escape

Adrian's ears were ringing. The pain shooting through his body awoke him from a state of unconsciousness. As he opened his eyes the horrors dawned upon him. He was surrounded by a cascade of dancing flames rising above the surface. In the centre of the madness though, was hope. The clear blue sky shone through the window above him. He needed air. Clear air. Adrian stumbled onto his feet and reached out to the window ledge. He leapt up quickly as he felt the heat spread. The only way out was to smash the window in front of him. Adrian took a deep breath. The fumes engulfed his lungs and sent him into a coughing fit. It was not his greatest idea. He looked around for any objects strong enough to smash the window. Nothing. Then, like a sign, the fire split. He could see his reflection in a narrow part of the window. He could use himself. Adrian put his shoulder forwards and pushed himself off the ground. As he collided with the window the glass smashed into small pieces, some now lodged into his skin. Adrian landed onto the concrete path outside. He faced the daytime sun. For a second it was like nothing ever happened. Then he looked across.

Spreading from the staff room the fire escalated through the bottom floor of the department unbalancing the structure of the school. Adrian watched the panicking staff and students barely managing to crawl out of the classroom. Still, he could hear nothing. Several of his classmates were still trapped inside. He had to help. Adrian stood up and faced the cauldron of fire once again. He peeked his head through the window he smashed and tried to find the remaining students. His hearing began to return as he heard the staff behind him screaming to stay away. Adrian just ignored them. Then at the corner of his eye he noticed his teacher Mrs Fletcher. He stepped inside and moved towards her. The temperature instantly increased. It became harder to breathe. Harder to move. But Adrian knew each second was precious. Battling the searing heat he could finally see Mrs Fletchers body drawing closer. He held her towards his chest and started to inch back towards the open window. The fire crackled around him as if it was mocking his struggles. But Adrian was tough. It was like his skin had grown an extra heat resistant layer. Within minutes he reached the window and climbed out. Waiting outside for him was a line of students and staff. They watched in awe as Adrian walked away from the fire with Mrs Fletcher in his arms. He set his teacher down and looked up at the people surrounding him.

"She's breathing but the fumes have knocked her out." The staff opened up their first aid kits and took her off Adrian.

Adrian took a longer look at the students who had escaped. Erik was at the front but someone else was missing.

"Where's Hannah…?" Adrian feared the answer.

Erik looked distraught as he stared down at Adrian. "I'm sorry mate. Nobody has seen her."

"She must be inside. I have to go!" Adrian's words were rushed and direct.

"What!? There's still a fire over there, you'll die!" But Erik's appeals were ignored. Adrian was already on his way back.

Adrian ran to the flames. Most of the classroom was in pieces, but the structure had miraculously held. Although Adrian knew he was minutes away from the top floor collapsing. Once he was inside the classroom he called out Hannah's name. Nothing. Adrian knew only one thing that would help him pinpoint her location. Where she was sat. He turned to his left and assessed the rubble that blocked the path. Adrian started searching by picking out the fallen bricks and burning tables. *Tables and chairs, I'm close.* Adrian started shifting the rubble at a faster pace. He could sense the presence of another person. He shouted Hannah's name again, a voice filled with pain and panic. Eventually he could see her. Lying peacefully on the ground surrounded by death was Hannah. Adrian had to act quickly. He grabbed her hand and pulled her out of the wreckage. Within seconds he leaped outside, successfully escaping the cauldron a third time. The audience gathered outside held their breath.

Adrian lay her down and checked her breathing. Nothing. He began pumping her chest in an attempt to resuscitate her. Hannah was not still not responding. After a couple of minutes Adrian ran out of breath. He took a short break and took as much air into his lungs as he could. Then he held her nose and breathed life back into her body. With a might breath of her own, Hannah perked up and awoke breathing heavily. Relieved, Adrian smiled. A shaken Hannah looked at her hero Adrian. The two of them made deep eye contact. In a second, she drew her lips towards Adrian's, kissing him.

Erik felt awkward but he had to interrupt. "Sorry you two lovebirds but there are still gunmen inside the school. It's still pretty dangerous. Certainly no time for kisses…"

Hannah turned to Adrian and smiled. "Sorry… but he has just saved my life."

Adrian stood up and turned to one of the teachers, Mr Evans. "How is Mrs Fletcher and the other students?" Adrian was clearly concerned.

"The students are okay. A few bruises but it's a miracle we got everyone out." Mr Evans's had a measured tone. "We have patched Mrs Fletcher up, she's awake now. The emergency services are on their way."

Adrian's attention turned to the gunmen still present inside the school. "Are there more gunman inside?"

Mr Evan's nodded. "I'm afraid so. As far as I'm aware they're in the staff room. There is still staff inside."

The deafening sound of a siren filled the empty air. Around three police cars and two ambulance vans arrived at the front entrance of the school. Mr Evans signalled to one of the ambulance vans to drive over. A man dressed in a green uniform climbed out the van and marched over to Mr Evans.

"I've been told you all have to move away from the area. If you follow me outside the premises I can treat everyone." Mr Evan's nodded and started to move everyone outside the school. Some students started to walk home while some gathered around hoping to get a glimpse of the drama that almost killed them. Adrian decided to stick with the staff.

The ambulance man and his driver lifted Mrs Fletcher onto the back of the van to treat her. Mrs Fletcher was awake but had not yet spoken so Mr Evans agreed to go to the hospital with her.

Officer Ruddy was the policeman that had taken charge of the situation. If Ruddy was not wearing his badge you would think he was one of the bad guys. His nasty character got results though. He was a man of strong

THE FRONT

authority and he took the law very seriously. The perfect fit for an intense situation like this. Ruddy had positioned the emergency units side by side. Each police car was perpendicular to the staff room to allowing the officers to shield themselves from any gunfire. There were around three officers to one car each armed with guns. Ruddy had already called in back up as with any hostage situation but he knew any action wouldn't wait. The first order of business was to catch up on any details. He searched the school grounds with a cold stare. He spotted the group of staff gathered at the entrance and decided to approach them.

"Afternoon, I'm Officer Ruddy and I'm in charge here. Can you please move away from the scene. Go home or to the pub I don't care. It's not safe here."

Surprisingly Adrian was the first to confront him. "Yes sir but–"

Ruddy looked down at Adrian with a confused expression. "You listen to me kid, no buts. I'm going to need an adult to stay with me; I... have a few questions."

Not giving up Adrian raised his voice. "I wanna stay... I can help."

Ruddy sighed and looked back at Adrian. "Stop wasting my time kid. My main priority right now is to keep as many people as I can away from harm. You will go home."

"C'mon Adrian it's not worth it," Erik replied, putting his hand on Adrian's back. "Let's go, they'll sort it out."

Ruddy smirked. "Listen to your friend kid."

Adrian started to walk away giving the Officer an angry stare whilst he passed. Erik and Adrian made their way half-way down the road until Hannah caught up with them.

"Adrian wait!"

The pair stopped. "Hannah, are you not off home?" Adrian replied.

"I'll walk with you, besides we never discussed lunch."

Erik rolled his eyes and raised his eyebrows towards Adrian.

"I thought we could talk in school tomorrow." Adrian was serious.

Hannah playfully giggled. "Don't be stupid Adrian, I doubt school will be open anytime soon. But I need to see you again."

Adrian laughed along. "All right... how about dinner tomorrow night?"

"Sounds lovely. I'll text you." Hannah stared into Adrian's eyes as they both shared a special moment.

But the moment was cut short. The air surrounding them became thin. A piercing sound echoed in the background. *Gunshots.*

"Shit that cop's down!" Erik yelled pointing to the fallen policeman.

"Both of you have to leave now!" Adrian screamed.

Erik knew exactly what Adrian was thinking. "No Adrian not again." Erik tried his best to convince Adrian to leave. "You can't stay, this isn't your place."

"Just go!" Adrian was not listening.

Hannah and Erik hurried down the road and turned the corner. Adrian looked back at the line of police cars. The smoke from the bullets blocked his view as he ran back towards the school blind. He could barely see the siren of the police car he was approaching. As he got closer he started to make out the human figures. One of his teachers Mr Berry was ducked behind one of the cars and another policemen was sat up against his car nurturing a wound at the top of his thigh. Adrian crouched to his knees to hide himself from any gunfire before taking cover at the same car.

A surprised Officer Ruddy greeted him. "What the hell are you doing back here kid?!" He was not impressed.

One Day

Officer Ruddy ignored Adrian's stare as he passed, instead choosing to focus on the situation at hand. The staff member that stayed with him was Mr Berry. One of the younger teachers. Mr Berry towered over Ruddy in comparison, something that secretly bothered the officer. *Not a looker*, Ruddy thought. He took Mr Berry behind the police cars inside the perimeter the officers had just mapped out. It stretched out to the end of the road and around the entire school.

"So, err… what exactly happened here?" The Officer scratched his head.

Mr Berry gave an honest account of what he had witnessed. "Well, I was teaching my geography class on the first floor near the entrance. I heard some shouting on the floor below that never usually happens."

"Really… no one shouts at these kids?" The officer grinned at himself. *Not the time for jokes.*

"No…" Mr Berry did not know what to think of the officer. "I left the classroom and approached the stairs, one at a time to see what was going on. Then I saw some guys in masks… balaclavas. I ran back to the first floor and raised the alarm. I told the students to use the stairwell at the other end. We met up with the other staff and students and got them as far away as we could. Then I saw Mrs Fletcher's English class explode and I ran over."

Officer Ruddy cut a stern figure, noting down the youthful teacher's words into his notebook. "What about the kids near the staff room?"

"They heard everything before us; the teachers had a look to see what was going on and when they realised what was happening they escaped through the windows. The gunmen were only present in two rooms."

"Do you know if anyone is still inside the staff room?"

Mr Berry shook his head. "I don't know for sure but we have to assume so. There are always at least two staff members on a break or free period in the staff room."

ONE DAY

Ruddy continued looking at this notepad and writing. He glanced up at the teacher with another question. "You mentioned an explosion at the English classroom, what happened there?"

"That was the other room where the gunmen took over. Apparently that student you spoke with, Adrian managed to overpower one of them and shoot the other two. After the explosion he lifted burning rubble to save a student and his teacher."

Ruddy raised his eyebrows "He shot two men?" The officer stopped making his notes and leaned forwards.

Mr Berry became uncomfortable and defensive. "I'm sure it was in self-defence, officer. You can't hold it against him."

Ruddy sniggered. "With the biggest respect Mr, I'll do my job how I see fit." Officer Ruddy glanced at Adrian, talking to Hannah at the end of the road.

"Do we know– "

Gunshots. Before Officer Ruddy could finish the gunmen burst through the entrance, firing bullets towards the police. He grabbed Mr Berry and forced him down behind Ruddy's police car. One of the officers next to them fell to the floor. Officer Ruddy saw a bullet lodged in his upper thigh.

"Goddamit Stevens stay with me!" But Ruddy knew he was helpless. The officer needed help but they did not have the man-power to deal with both situations. He needed a miracle.

Emerging from the smoke that filled the air, the figure of student Adrian leaped next to the wounded Stevens. Officer Ruddy had to catch his breath.

"What the hell are you doing back here kid?!" Ruddy became even more anxious.

"You looked like you needed some help." Adrian could not help but grin at the angry officer.

Ruddy shrugged. "It's your own life on the line."

Adrian turned his attention to the wounded officer. He saw the bullet lodged in his thigh and pulled it out. The officer recoiled in pain.

"Hey kid, wait… what's your name?"

"Adrian, sir."

THE FRONT

"Adrian take my gun, you're more useful than me right now." The officer handed Adrian the loaded pistol. He cradled it in the palms of his hands and stared at it for a few moments. The officer watched. "Don't worry, I trust you. Here, take my vest too, in case... god forbid... you get shot."

Adrian held out the pistol and declined the offer. "Thanks sir but I have to get you to safety."

"Forget that, I can take care of myself. But there are people behind these cars that need your help." Adrian took back the gun and pulled on the bullet-proof vest. An officer of the law who he only just met had faith in him. This was the least he could do. Officer Stevens opened the car door and grabbed a first aid pack. The gunshots stopped. Adrian patiently awaited his orders.

"On the count of three," Ruddy whispered.

On three the officers lifted themselves above the cars, holding their guns towards their opponents. Before them stood four gunmen, three of them holding guns to the heads of the school staff.

"Shoot and we will kill all of them. All you have to do is let us go." The gunman who spoke stood in front of the others. His voice had a foreign hint to it.

"You know we can't do that." Ruddy replied, standing firm. "You're outnumbered."

The gunman was not backing down. "Drop your weapons and clear the area."

Adrian could see all three hostages had cuts and blood running down their faces. Two of the gunmen were holding black sacks behind their back, presumably filled with cash. Officer Ruddy started to receive information from his ear piece from the department.

"A helicopter is close to you, further ground back up in six minutes."

We don't have six minutes, Ruddy thought.

"You have a minute until we kill them." A healthy reminder echoed around the scene.

"Hey kid, a helicopter is on its way soon. Do you have any ideas?" Ruddy whispered to Adrian.

Adrian looked bewildered. "Wait... you don't have a plan?"

"He's got our hands tied and he doesn't look like the kind of guy who wants to negotiate."

Adrian started to look around. "I'll go over there. Try to talk to them… Just make sure you can take them down if you have to."

Officer Ruddy shook his head in disagreement. "You know I can't allow that!"

"Apparently you don't have another option!" Adrian stared at the anxious officer. "Trust me; I know what I'm doing."

Officer Ruddy sighed. Adrian was right. His hands were tied. But first he needed to clear something up. "Is it true you saved the students in your class?"

Adrian's expression gave nothing away. "Just trust me." The teenager was reluctant.

Devoid of any other last minute plans, Ruddy nodded and whispered his orders to the team. "Okay men I want guns on the three gunmen with hostages, do not shoot until I give the order."

Adrian slipped a smoke grenade from the injured officer behind his neck and stood up. He climbed over the police car and inched towards the gunmen before stopping and placing his gun on the floor.

"What do you think you are doing boy?" The gunman asked directing his gun towards Adrian.

"I just want to talk." Adrian placed his hands behind his head. "You wouldn't fire at an unarmed kid, would you?"

"You would be surprised." The gunman replied. Adrian could feel the gunman sneering underneath his mask.

Overhead the helicopter had finally arrived. The thunderous noise distracted the attention of all four gunmen, an opportunity engineered by Adrian. Now he just had to take it. He pulled out the smoke grenade and rolled it towards the gunmen and hostages. The three hostages pulled away from the confused gunmen as the smoke made them virtually invisible. The gunmen started to fire bullets wherever they could completely blind to their surroundings. Adrian leaped towards the lead gunman and landed a painful blow on his head. He then hit another in the stomach, using his weight to spin around his body and kick the other two. As the smoke cleared the marksmen opened their eyes to police officers pointing guns at them from point blank range.

The scene fell silent. The defeated gunmen pulled down their masks and put their hands up. The relieved officers grabbed their wrists and tightly handcuffed them together. Officer Ruddy stood proud holding his belt buckle whilst he watched his men throw the arsonists into the back of the police vans. He decided to approach a shaken Adrian.

"Good quick thinking out there son. What's your name again?"

Adrian peered above still catching his breath. "Adrian sir."

"Adrian, we are going to need some further information on the events today and the part you had to play. But it can wait." Officer Ruddy broke a smile. Ruddy held out his hand.

Adrian shook it and nodded. "Thank you, sir."

Adrian rubbed the palm of his hand down his face. The school grounds were crowded with people and vehicles. Ambulance staff ran past him at full pelt. The lights of the sirens still shone, like the pulse of a beating heart. Adrian began his journey home alone. He was still alive. But he had a feeling his life just changed forever.

Sinaloa Cartel

Just one light bulb hung off the ceiling in the centre of the room. It offered barely no light. The room had no windows and only one door. At one side was a metal table with old papers, coats and a back-pack placed on top. There was also an open first aid kit on the floor next to which lay a man with his back to the wall. He was clutching his right arm where a large piece of glass had pieced into his skin. With a clenched fist he used his left hand to pluck the piece of glass out slowly and carefully. He gritted his teeth and closed his eyes before anguishing in pain. Once out, he chucked the glass to one side and reached into the first aid kit. Blood started seeping out onto the floor.

He searched through the kit, pulling out a needle and some suture thread. He took a deep breath and poked the needle into one side of the wound. Small areas of the wound started to close up with a cross stitch until the end of the wound was reached. After another scuffle into the first aid kit, he rolled a white bandage around his arm and wiped the blood off his hands using an old rag. He rested his head back onto the wall and relaxed his muscles, in an attempt to overcome the ordeal he just faced. But there wasn't much time to relax. The door burst open, only just managing to hang onto its hinges. In the doorway stood a slightly larger man, wearing a white lined black suit and holding a cigarette in his mouth. With one puff he withdrew the cigarette and started talking.

"Simon you bastard! What the hell happened!?" His Mexican accent was prominent from his dominant and loud tone.

One of the most notorious criminals in America, Roberto Salazar was famous for his tough exterior and lack of remorse. He was feared by most communities and gangs in the neighbourhood and beyond. Salazar was born in a low-income community bought up only by his father who was part of the local gang named Sinaloa Cartel. This meant Salazar had no other option but to join him. When he was 16, he had to undergo an initiation to prove his loyalty and commitment to the group.

THE FRONT

The gang attracted a police officer to a nearby desolate park. Salazar hid behind the wall of a small crumbling structure. The police man arrived in the centre of his view. He looked around, confused and lost. Like a sitting duck. Once the policeman was facing away from him, Salazar jumped out holding a full tang hunting knife. Its blade was thick and its handle curved. Before the police officer could react Salazar launched the knife into his back. His spine was instantly damaged and one of his lungs tore open. Blood leaked out of the officer's mouth as his knees fell to the floor. He lay unconscious and impaired on the pavement of the park pathway. Salazar stood over him, proud and accomplished. He withdrew the blood-soaked knife from his back and walked away.

Salazar was now in his late 30's and one of the senior members of the gang, taking up his father's position since his death. Sinaloa Cartel had expanded its operations into multiple countries and cities including New York. Salazar chose to work in New York continuing the gang's activities. He lived in Pittsburgh away from any operations that could land him in prison. Each member of his New York crew was devoted and loyal. They all knew what would happen to them otherwise.

"It's that damn kid! He sprung up, shot Ed and before I knew it the place blew to bits." Simon continued to hold onto his wounded arm.

Salazar flicked his cigarette onto the floor. He stared at Simon. "What kid? You're telling me I've lost two of my team members because of a child?"

"You weren't there!" Simon dropped his head and began a solitary tone of voice.

Simon was one of Salazar's devoted members. He was one of only a few people Salazar trusted. Simon was recruited from New York City from a broken community. With no prospects and no one to care, he joined a local gang after they tried to rob him. Being part of a gang gave him an identity, a status. He was given recognition from his fellow gang members and was around people that wanted to protect him. In turn, he helped them steal from his own parents. They took everything they had; their car, their money and any jewellery they could find. Since then he left his family and stayed with some of the gang members.

"This... This is dangerous. This game we're playing is a dangerous game. And it's only gone downhill since Peter."

The mention of the name irked Salazar. "We are not stopping now!"

"We've lost everyone can you not see that! I was the only one that survived!"

"So...what? What other option do we have?"

Salazar paused in thought for a moment. It seemed everything had been spoilt by one person.

"He's the one that took it all away from us." Simon responded. He knew exactly what Salazar was thinking. "We have to do what the others would have wanted."

Salazar took more time in thought as Simon's words lingered in the room. "He took away your everything. Your *Ella*. This isn't just any kid. He's dangerous. So, what are you going to do?" Simon climbed to his feet and looked down at his leader.

When Sinaloa Cartel began to expand their operations, they sought after new recruits inside existing local gangs. Simon was chosen and taken under Salazar's wing as a close advisor. He knew the local area and the gang culture well. He also had the drive and the will to succeed and gave all he had to the organisation. Simon was also a close observer of Salazar's lust for co-worker Ella. Ella joined the gang four years ago following in the footsteps of her husband. At first, he had doubts about whether the group would be accepting of a female member, but she was a strong girl. She almost never showed any emotion. Eventually they let her in, trained her up and assigned her missions. She adapted to life quite well considering the culture change having developed close friendships with some gang members including Simon and staying close to her husband.

The business Sinaloa Cartel ran in New York varied but it was not always like that. At first they focused on drug trafficking and organised crime such as hit jobs. Recently however, they had moved to darker crimes like sex trafficking and supplying for Islamic terrorist organisations. They were also involved in money-laundering to help them all share a healthy profit. Joint operations by the Mexican and US government shut down a large portion of the gang's activities as they seized around 2 tonnes of cocaine and 60 million dollars' worth of property, making multiple arrests.

Their lack of financial intelligence lead the authorities straight to them. Salazar and his gang had always managed to escape any of this as the police efforts were focused away from home territory. They changed base every month and altered their identities regularly. With local American's in their group they could fit in well without anyone taking notice of them.

The gang still had communications with Sinaloa Cartel members in America and Mexico but they knew they had been left isolated. Their business now was to survive and escape capture. They had enough funds to sustain a group for a decade, maybe more but they had no intention of running any major drug operations. It would be very high risk. With the death of two gang members and the arrest of four more the gang were down to limited numbers. Only four senior members remained including Salazar and Simon. The whole group was close-knit, reliable and dependable. It was a necessity if they were to survive as a unit and avoid capture.

Salazar stopped thinking. He moved in closer to Simon. "We kill the kid." Simon nodded in agreement.

Only time would tell whether they would be successful.

First Date

Adrian opened his dreary eyes. The morning sun was shining through the window behind him drowning out the stars on his ceiling. He had only managed to sleep for the last three hours. The images of the gunmen holding his life at the tip of their guns had replayed through his mind all night. Adrian sat upright at the side of his bed looking across his room. His school uniform was sprawled across the dark blue carpet with blood stains reflecting in the sunlight. Across his desk was his school work and his laptop. Next to that was a chest of drawers and his wardrobe stood in the corner in front of his bed. Adrian usually kept his room tidy. It helped him organise his mind. The decoration of his room had not changed. Three walls painted white and one red diamond coated wall facing his bed.

Adrian's mum came home an hour after Adrian, once the school had told her what happened. Her first instinct was to wrap her arms around him like she was wrapping him in a blanket. It took a long time for her to let go. Mrs Leones then poured herself a drink and sat down opposite Adrian. Adrian felt uncomfortable telling his mother the whole story. She was angry when it emerged he stood up to gunmen in the classroom to protect his classmates. Adrian had nothing more to say. Fire and blood. That is all he could see. But the scene was not the only thing he was thinking about. *How will people react to me? How will this change what my friends think about me?*

A bright light flashed onto the ceiling. Adrian reached over and grabbed his phone. It was a text from Hannah.

"Hey, are we still on for tonight? Xxx"

If Adrian was to take anything positive from the day before, it was Hannah. His first date was on the horizon. Adrian did not know how long his date with the police would last though. There was a chance he could spend the night there. This date was the only hope Adrian had of being himself again, at least for another night. He tapped a message into his phone and placed it back onto his desk. He had a big day to prepare for.

THE FRONT

Officer Ruddy was sat next to Mrs Leones in her kitchen. Whilst waiting for Adrian he engaged in light conversation with his mother. But Ruddy quickly realised she was not in the mood.

"Adrian didn't do anything wrong. This will just be routine."

Mrs Leones had her back turned to the officer. She quietly sniffed and rubbed her eyes. In the corner of his eye he spotted an irritated Adrian making his way down the stairs. Adrian acknowledged him before pouring himself some cereal and milk and a glass of orange juice. Adrian glanced at his mother but stayed silent and carried on eating. He knew he could not make the situation any better. Once he was finished eating, the officer led him outside and into the back seat of a police car. It was the first time he had been in a police car. Adrian lay his head on the door window and had a thought. The person driving him today may not have survived if it was not for his own intervention and yet Adrian found himself caught up the mess. As he watched his home disappear through the window Adrian knew one thing. There was a price to being a hero.

* * *

Adrian found himself in a dull and lifeless grey room. He was sat on one of the four chairs surrounding a brown wooden table with a standing microphone angled towards him. The room was only lit by a central light hanging from the ceiling. It seemed like the room had been designed to give a taster of prison to any potential inmates. Adrian was soon joined by two police detectives, Will Sampson and Malcolm Stone.

Will was the first to speak. "Good afternoon Mr Leones. We just want to ask you some questions okay?" His voice was calm and smooth.

Adrian nodded. Detective Stone turned on the microphone and confirmed some details.

"Thirteen thirteen on eleventh September 2012" The date was all too familiar to Americans. Then came the details from the crime scene.

"What occurred, in your experience Mr Leones at the time of the incident on 10/09/2012?"

Adrian shifted in his seat. "Three people... with guns came into the classroom. They... shouted things. Get down on the floor, stuff like that. They threatened my teacher, Mrs Fletcher."

"Why did they threaten Mrs Fletcher?"

FIRST DATE

"She wouldn't stay down. Then there was this explosion... all I can remember was waking up afterwards. The whole room had collapsed in on itself." Adrian became increasingly uneasy.

"Are you sure there were three active gunmen?" Will started to press the issue.

A surprised Adrian became more direct with his answers. "There was definitely three of them"

"How can you be certain? You were face down at the time."

Adrian could feel the increased intensity from the detective. "I watched them stand at three different points." Adrian knew his point was valid but he found himself being defensive.

The detectives took a moment to make notes. Detective Sampson then changed the line of questioning. "What happened after the explosion?"

"I got out of the building and helped Mrs Fletcher out. I managed to pull some other students from the fire too. Then the police and ambulance arrived."

Adrian's words lingered for a few moments. To his relief, a policeman entered the room and summoned the two detectives. They told Adrian to wait before following the policeman outside. Adrian used this time to collect his thoughts. *Do they know what else happened in the classroom? They have not mentioned the incident with the police yet either. Officer Ruddy would have told them about that wouldn't he?* After half an hour of waiting alone the two detectives re-joined Adrian looking concerned. They took their places opposite Adrian contemplating their next move.

This time Malcolm decided to speak. "Mr Leones, we have just received some information regarding the post-mortem done on the gunman. Are you sure there isn't anything else you would like to tell us?"

"...Yes." Adrian held firm.

"Mr Leones... We found gunshot wounds on the body we recovered. I must remind you that you could face heavier consequences if you decide to... hide things from us."

Adrian didn't move. The odds now seemed stacked against him. Yet something told him to hang on. *Play the game a bit longer.* Adrian relaxed himself and stared at the detective deep into his eyes before asking a simple question.

THE FRONT

"Any more questions officer?"

Malcolm looked rattled. The detective stood up as an attempt to intimidate the teenager. He rested his palms on the table and gave Adrian a stern look.

"With reason to believe you're lying to us, we can detain you."

Unmoved, Adrian continued to challenge the detective.

"You and I both know with no evidence you have no right to keep me here." Adrian felt the pendulum swing to his favour.

A sly grin grew on Malcolm's face. "Who said we don't have any evidence?"

Adrian's face dropped. The game just got serious.

After a silent moment, he replied. "I want a lawyer."

The detectives nodded. "You're going to have to contact your mother. I'm assuming you don't have your own lawyer?"

Adrian shook his head. He followed the detectives outside towards a phone. Panic started to set into his mood. *What evidence?* In truth there were many things the police could have gotten hold of. Adrian had lost control of the situation. He doubted whether he ever was in control. The worst part about not being in control is not knowing what will happen next.

* * *

'They'll be in touch." Sounding shaken and mentally bruised, Adrian's mother felt she was reaching worst case scenario. She was surprised it had gotten this far. Only hope would get her and Adrian through this. Somehow.

Adrian felt deflated. As he hooked the phone back up, his posture weakened and everything started to catch up with him. No longer was he filled with any adrenaline, any rushed decisions. It was just him and darker thoughts. Two officers ushered Adrian into a waiting room next to the main entrance to the station. Hours passed by as Adrian and the detectives waited for his lawyer to turn up. Adrian glanced at his watch. *2:08*. He had agreed to meet Hannah at 7. *I have to make it.* Adrian's eyes were fixated onto the floor as he could not find the energy to lift up his head. He knew he had let his mum down. Her voice sounded broken and Adrian felt her pain on the other end. But he had to get through this. As Adrian lifted up his head he caught the sight of one of the detectives, Malcolm. Malcolm was deep in conversation with another officer. One Adrian recognised well.

Officer Ruddy faced a moral dilemma. He knew the law. He knew what his role as a police officer meant. He knew the responsibilities he held. But he witnessed Adrian's heroics that day. *Does he lie to his colleagues to save Adrian? Surly the police would make the right decision if they had all the information?* He started to pace around the station, looking for Will or Malcolm in charge of the investigation. The officer reached the waiting room behind the main reception area of the station. The double doors at the back of the room lead to some of the main offices. The chairs were organised as a circle in the middle of the room running in parallel with chairs against the walls. There, sat in the corner was teenager Adrian. His head was down and he looked deep in thought.

"Malcolm!" Officer Ruddy stopped the fast-moving detective as he passed through the waiting room.

"I have more information."

Malcolm stared curiously at the officer. "This better be worth my time."

Ruddy took a breath. "Adrian... He had to stop them... them criminals from harming anyone. I don't know the full details but please, he only has good intentions."

Malcolm raised his eyebrows. "Officer, would you be prepared to make another statement for us?"

* * *

Adrian now had company but he still felt isolated. Next to him sat Jack Quinn, family lawyer to the Leones. Mr Quinn had a tall slim build with mid-shaven facial hair. His attitude was professional, one that offered little comfort for Adrian. Before the detectives entered the room, Mr Quinn offered Adrian some advice.

"I know this is tough. You don't have to answer any questions. I am here to fight your corner, all right?" His tone was quiet and reserved.

Adrian nodded. Calmly, Will and Malcolm entered the room. The duo were both holding folders at their side. Both unbuttoned their blazers as they took their seats.

"Five twelve, the eleventh of September 2013. Present is fellow detective Will Sampson, suspect Adrian Leones and lawyer Jack Quinn and myself Malcolm Stone."

Will began to lay out the details. "It seems, Mr Leones, more details have emerged from the incident your involved in. Is there anything you would like to say before we start to bring these to your attention?" He leaned over and watched Adrian as he reacted to the news.

Everyone in the room waited for a reply. "No." Adrian could not have been more straightforward.

"Mr Leones, a gun was recovered from the classroom you were in. It has your fingerprint's on."

Adrian sat forward. His pulse started to race.

"However, Mr Leones, we received this statement from an internal body who was at the scene."

Malcolm reached into his folder and pulled out a file. He slid it over to Mr Quinn. Adrian glanced over.

"Wait, this is from Officer Ruddy." Adrian was surprised.

"Yes, you seem to know each other well." Will responded.

"This statement works in our favour. Adrian acted in self-defence, for himself, the staff and the students. You don't have any grounds to take him in." Mr Quinn instantly shot down the detective's attempts to accuse Adrian.

"Exactly Mr Quinn. Adrian's actions were clearly in self-defence. His assistance to the police was necessary and welcome. His intentions were good."

Adrian felt the relief spread across his body. His shoulders dropped and the tension cleared from his head.

"Congratulations Adrian. You're free to go." Mr Quinn was the first to offer Adrian his hand as they both stood up.

"Thanks for the help."

Adrian then gave Will Sampson a handshake and offered his hand to Malcolm Stone. With a firm grip Malcolm looked into Adrian's eyes and pulled him closer.

He leant in and whispered into Adrian's ear. "Don't ever try to lie to me again."

FIRST DATE

Adrian backed away. This had been a bitter sweet victory.

*   *   *

Adrian watched his house come into view as the Lexus car pulled up outside his house. His lawyer Jack Quinn had generously offered him a lift home. As he climbed out of the car he faced his sunset lit house. He barely took two steps inside before his mother emerged from the hall and embraced him. He rested his head on his mother's shoulder and started to shed tears. For a moment Adrian could let his emotions free.

"I miss Dad." Adrian whispered.

Mrs Leones held that little bit tighter. Adrian let go and stood back. He used both his hands to wipe away the tears from his eyes and gathered his thoughts once more.

"Sorry, I have to go."

Mrs Leones was confused. "Where?"

Adrian broke a smile. "I have a date."

Street Lights

Down the 10th Street Bypass stood a girl. Her name was Hannah Park. She was 16, fair build with stunning brown hair running down to her shoulders. She waited patiently clutching a small black and gold bag. She wore a sapphire coloured dress that complimented her down to her knees. This was a special occasion. She looked across the river and gazed at the city as the sun set, a symphony of orange and red colours. The day was almost over. The street light above her lit up and Hannah caught the sight of Adrian in the distance. The night had just begun.

"You look beautiful." Adrian's words were soft and sincere. Hannah, flattered, smiled and acknowledged the gesture.

"I'm sorry I didn't bring anything. I only had time to make sure I smelt nice!" Adrian nervously laughed.

"You smell lovely. The important thing is that you're here." Hannah calmed his nerves. "So, where are we going?"

Adrian pointed across the boulevard to Alihan's Mediterranean Cuisine on 6th Street. Hannah held his hand as they walked to the restaurant.

Adrian approached the staff member at the front as they entered.

"Hi my name is Adrian Leones, I booked a table for two this morning." The waiter looked up at Adrian and a smile grew over his face.

"Ah Adrian, welcome welcome! Your table is right over here." He took Adrian and Hannah over to the end of the restaurant where their sea view table was waiting. Before he left them he handed over the menus and whispered in Hannah's ear.

"You must be special."

Hannah instinctively smiled, not knowing how to react.

Adrian laughed. "Cheeky waiter!"

The restaurant was not large. This was not a premium restaurant, but Adrian had heard the food was nice and the atmosphere suited the night he had in mind. The restaurant was simply designed. Square white tables and cushioned chairs filled the main area complemented by a warm yellow glow from the walls. A large chandelier hung from the ceiling in the centre of the restaurant, a spherical two tiered light fixture that dominated the room.

Once settled Adrian and Hannah stared at each other for a moment before Adrian broke the ice. "So, tell me about yourself?"

As the evening went on the couple looked more comfortable around one another. As soon as the awkward conversations were over, the topic moved onto recent events.

"I still don't think I've thanked you enough for yesterday." Hannah took a sip of her drink.

Adrian gave her a noble response. "Hannah, this is enough. Just being here now, it's enough"

"Everyone was amazed at what you did. I don't think they expected you to be the one to stand up."

Adrian shrugged his shoulders. "Well, sometimes people are underestimated."

"Tell me about it! You took them out like a professional." Hannah looked around and leaned in towards Adrian. "Where... When did you learn how to do that?"

Adrian followed. "I think I have always had it in me. Somehow, I feel different."

"What do you mean?" Hannah whispered.

Adrian felt unsettled. He quietly laughed to himself before relaxing back into his chair. "It... it doesn't matter. I don't want to talk about it."

Hannah sensed the mood change and looked sympathetically towards Adrian. "What river is that anyway? Pittsburgh is surrounded by them."

"Do you not listen in Geography?" Adrian lifted his head and grinned.

Hannah looked surprised. "Insight me then special one!"

"That's the Allegheny River, one of three rivers that run through Pittsburgh. It comes down from the North East and meets the Ohio River running from the North West." Adrian felt silly saying it out loud.

Hannah was hooked onto every word Adrian uttered. When he was finished she paused for a moment, speechless.

"Adrian that's amazing. You're really bright. I want to know more of this Adrian."

Adrian would not admit that made him feel special. "It's just general knowledge, I live here. So do you!"

Hannah laughed. "This isn't about me! I don't remember that kind of stuff."

Adrian raised his eyebrows. "So what do you know about?"

"How about you wait until we get outside, when the stars are out." The couple simultaneously smiled at one another.

"I guess we'll have to skip dessert then!"

Adrian and Hannah both split the bill and left the restaurant. The night had now graced the city and the lights from the streets, skyscrapers and bridges have taken over. Adrian started walking Hannah back to her house near the quieter streets with fewer lights.

Hannah stopped. "See that star over there? The brightest one in the night sky."

Adrian followed Hannah's finger pointing at the sky. "Yeah, near the moon."

"That's not a star. It's Jupiter. You know... Jupiter is my favourite planet."

"Why's that?"

"It's the biggest planet in our Solar System. It's a big powerful giant. Yet, between the lines, I can see its beauty. Storms that produce the colours of dreams. An atmosphere that is more alive than ours."

Now Adrian was the one that was speechless. "Hannah, that's... that's wonderful."

The pair continued walking on. As they passed the empty streets, Adrian noticed one street with a broken light. He stopped and stared into the darkness. Hannah was curious and stopped beside him.

Adrian looked into Hannah's eyes. "Did you ever hear the story of the street lights in Pittsburgh?"

"No." Hannah replied.

Adrian took a deep breath. "There once was a street in this city. It was full of old abandoned houses. In the daytime, the sun would light it up and it would just seem so dark... and empty. At night though, it would literally be dark. All the street lights were broken. Then, one night, a man was walking his dog and to his surprise, he saw light. In the middle of the street, just one street light had lit up."

Adrian stopped. He held out his hands with his palms up, signalling for Hannah to place hers on top. Adrian continued with the story.

"The strange thing was, in that miraculous light, he saw his wife. She smiled at him and then faded away. His wife had been dead for five years. People thought he was mad. I know he wasn't. Because whenever I see a street light at night, I see the person I miss the most. He's there. Smiling."

Hannah let go of his hands and wrapped her arms around him.

"You're a strong person Adrian. To get through these last couple of years takes strength." Hannah stepped back and took hold of his hands again.

Adrian looked sorrowfully at Hannah. "Thanks. I always wonder, every day. Would he be proud of me? What would he think about the person I've become?"

Hannah consoled the sorry teenager. "Course he would! Adrian, you saved my life."

She grabbed his hand and dragged him through the last few blocks. As they reached her house, Hannah reflected on the night.

"Adrian, tonight has been fun. Thanks for taking me out. We should do this again."

"I've had a good night too. Except my breakdown. Are you sure you want to see me again?" Adrian nervously laughed along with what he hoped was a funny joke.

"Sure I do." Hannah stopped. She stared lovingly into Adrian's eyes and moved closer. Her palms rested on his cheeks and her lips caressed his. After a precious moment she pulled away and left Adrian grinning with joy.

He watched Hannah disappear into her house and carried on smiling.

Missing

Two Years Ago. Mrs Leones had not seen her husband all day. She had woken up in an empty bed. She had a feeling something was not quite right. It had happened before. She would wake up alone often. But this was different. She sat in near darkness on a single sofa swirling a glass of wine, frequently peering at the clock. The only light came from a table lamp in the corner of the room. It had just gone six in the evening and there had been no sign of her husband returning from work. There was no sign of Adrian either. The clock she was staring at was large, with roman numerals instead of numbers telling the time. Below the clock was the fireplace, where some of the family photos were displayed. The family looked joyful on Adrian's tenth birthday. Life had become uncertain since then.

The door handle began to shake. Mrs Leones held her breath. But she was disappointed. It was Adrian. He shut the door behind him, dropped his bag and stayed by the doorway. Looking at his mother he simply asked;

"Where's Dad?"

Mrs Leones responded in the simplest way she could. "He's not here yet."

Adrian lumbered up to his bedroom.

She considered whether she was being too harsh on her son. She had not even asked him where he had been so late. But Adrian had been asking too many questions recently. Keeping Adrian at a distance kept him safer. They were protecting him. Although the thought she could be on her own crossed her mind. It was a chilling thought. In her eyes, he had to return soon. She moved into the kitchen and called Adrian down for dinner. She served it up and they sat side by side as they ate. The half-lit room stayed silent. Mrs Leones uttered the first, forced words.

"Why were you late today?" Her tone suggested it was not the first time.

Adrian brushed it off. "I stayed behind at school. Me and Erik did some Maths work after class."

"For two hours! I hardly believe that."

Adrian looked flustered. "I went back to his for a while. Where is Dad anyway?"

The question sent tingles through her body. "He just hasn't turned up yet okay."

The room was brought to silence. Mrs Leones reached out her hand and placed it on Adrian's. She could see the worry in his eyes. She was worried too, but she could not show it. She felt she had to stay strong for Adrian's sake. Now was not the time for the truth. Once they had both finished dinner they placed their plates at the side of the sink and followed each other up the stairs, before going their own way. Adrian said a solitary 'goodnight' to his mother and disappeared into his room. He rested his head on his pillow and lay in his bed. Pulling the covers up to his neck, he started to think about his father. He still had questions.

In the other room, Mrs Leones lay in her bed with the same thoughts. She knew she was not going to be able to get any sleep. Her mind was too active. As all the questions circulated around her head, panic started to creep in. It was a heart sinking moment. She felt weightless. Sat up in her bed she grabbed her phone on the bedside table and frantically dialled her husband's number. It rang. No answer. She tried again. The ringing took her to voicemail. As she heard his message she moved her mobile towards her chest. Her eyes started to fill with tears. A helpless feeling drew over her.

Sorry I can't take your call at the moment, please call back later or leave a message.

She could not stop hearing his voice inside her head. All the doubt, all the uncertainty, all the pain. It all combined to make her world stop. Stop for her. There was no moving forward. There would be no tomorrow.

* * *

Adrian stared into his living area. His mother and two police officers were discussing his father's disappearance. *Was it out of character? Did he have any threats?* Adrian had only slept for a couple of hours. He could hear his mother next door all night, shuffling her blankets and making regular trips downstairs. He knew he may have seen the last of his father.

As the police left Adrian approached his mother. "What did they say?"

Mrs Leones ignored him and moved towards the kitchen. At no point did she look at him or register his existence. He basically got the cold shoulder. But Adrian could understand her silence, understand her pain. At this moment, she was in a world of her own. Even he was struggling to comprehend the situation. He did feel, however, that a situation like this meant they should be closer to each other, helping each other although he did not want to raise that issue just yet. He wanted to give his mother more space, more time to deal with her grievance.

Mrs Leones had gotten no sleep the night before. The police were not made aware of the full story but they knew enough to try and find him. She had given the police an old photograph of her husband. No doubt she would see it on 'Missing' posters across the town. She was not comfortable with that thought, but she was prepared to sacrifice her emotions to get him back. Her world had stopped spinning. She needed her life back. As she poured herself a cup of tea, there was a knock at the door. She waited by the kitchen doorway as Adrian answered it. It was her mother and her sister along with her husband and their son. They embraced Adrian first before moving towards the kitchen. Mrs Leones could see her mother holding some Tupperware with food inside. After she shared a sympathetic look with her family they each gave her a hug whilst Adrian kept his distance.

Mrs Leones' sister Caroline was a few years younger than herself. She had a similar complexion, dark hair and slim build. She was always complemented on her smile, one Mrs Leones' envied. Caroline was always positive, a quality that drew people towards her. Mrs Leones often found herself a recluse because of it.

"They will find him." Her tone, although meant to be comforting, sounded patronising to Mrs Leones. She offered a small forced smile and a nod in return.

They moved to the living room and took their places on the sofas. Mrs Leones offered up the tea she just made. Adrian sat on the end of the sofa, the furthest from his mother. The atmosphere was fragile. Adrian's grandmother Isabel was the first to break the silence.

"So Adrian, how is school going?"

"Okay, nothing new." Adrian was not sure how to respond to such a vague question, especially as he watched his mother give him a dark stare.

"How are you coping Adrian?" Caroline made the conversation more serious. Mrs Leones' eyes were still fixed on Adrian.

"I think he'll come home." Adrian replied in an optimistic tone. It was met with an unnoticeable hiss from his mother. But Adrian did notice it.

After a moment of more silence, Caroline suggested Adrian took her son upstairs while they spoke to Mrs Leones. Adrian agreed and took him to his room. The adults stayed gathered around the sofas. Caroline made an observation towards Mrs Leones.

"It seems you're being a little distant towards Adrian."

Mrs Leones now seemed flustered. "How dare you! The last thing on my mind right now is to ignore my own son. I don't have the mind to think about anything else right now."

Caroline sat forward. "I understand that. I just think talking to Adrian will help you deal with this situation. Don't you agree?" Caroline opened the question out to the room. Her mother nodded.

"Adrian doesn't care. You see how he reacts. I don't see how he could help me."

"Adrian cares. It's his father. He is going through exactly the same as you. He is just dealing with it in a different way."

Mrs Leones seemed to accept Caroline's stance. She dropped her head and produced no response. For the first time she thought about the family around her, especially Adrian. Inside, Adrian would be hurting just as much as her.

Upstairs, Adrian and Caroline's son Harrison were playing Call of Duty on Adrian's Xbox. Harrison was 12 years old, a few years younger than Adrian.

"How's big school then Harrison?" Adrian continued to keep an upbeat mood.

Harrison shrugged. "It's okay."

It was the typical blunt reply Adrian expected.

"What do you think happened to Uncle Peter?" Adrian shuddered. He hadn't heard his father's name for a while.

"I don't know but I am sure he will be back."

Harrison paused his game and put the controller down. "How can you be so sure?"

"To be honest I'm not. But in these situations you have to be hopeful. That's all you can be. That hope is what's getting me and my mother through the day and maybe the days." Adrian gave a reply his cousin deserved.

Harrison nodded and turned his focus back on the video game.

* * *

A few days had passed. Peter had still not turned up and there was no sightings of him from the police or the public. The campaign aimed at finding him started to lose its momentum. The police were slowly giving up hope. Adrian and his mother were left isolated with their thoughts and each other. Adrian found himself getting closer to his mother over the past few days as she started to come to terms with Peter's disappearance. They were both still without answers though and that was the worst part. Mrs Leones struggled to comprehend the idea that someone so close to her could just disappear so quickly, with no trace.

Adrian had not returned to school nor has Mrs Leones returned to work. Instead they spent their days at home assisting with the campaign and the police investigation. They had been outside only a couple of times to attempt a physical search, but their minds were never in the right place. For every person they glanced at they thought it could be Peter. Being in public places messed with their heads. Their days and nights were quiet. During the day they would keep an eye on the news and the internet. In the evenings they would eat, watch TV and go to bed. Not that they were getting any sleep however. Their grievance was still young, the mystery still unsolved. They were both very much grounded in the moment. Years of pain had only just begun.

Don't Look Down

Pittsburgh High School was slowly returning back to normality. It had been four weeks since gunmen stormed the school, took hostages and attempted robbery. But finally the school reopened to students and the remaining staff. The front and western side of the school had been rebuilt after the explosion. The classrooms still had the smell of fresh paint and new carpets. The head teacher had gathered all the staff together in the staff room for an important conversation. The staff were already engrossed in talks about the incident. Some of the staff had near death experiences. Some had almost witnessed the death of their students.

The voices turned to silence as the head teacher entered the room. "First of all, welcome back to the high school. Some of the staff here and the construction workers have worked tirelessly to get the school back to the way it was and open so soon. To them I say thank you. It means a lot less hassle for the pupils and their parents."

He continued with a more serious tone.

"The students will most definitely have questions. Answer them as you wish but consider your responsibilities. Make it clear that we do not intend for a similar situation to happen again, that this was an isolated incident and this school is still a safe place to learn. Thank you and once again, welcome back."

The staff all dispatched to their classrooms to begin a day of work.

Adrian gazed up at the school as he approached. That was all he could do. If he looked anywhere else he would make eye contact with all the students staring at him. He was the talk of the school. The students were surprised by Adrian's actions and had become cautious of him. Erik spotted Adrian walking with his head up and caught up with him.

"Adrian, what are you looking at?"

Adrian heard Erik's familiar voice. He angled down his neck and started rubbing it. "Oh hey Erik, it's stupid. Everyone's looking at me."

"What did you expect? You're a hero!"

THE FRONT

Adrian sighed. "I don't think they quite see it in the same way…"

They both stuck together as they arrived at their first lesson, Geography. Adrian noticed the walls of the corridor were bare. It was more comparative to a criminal institution than a school. The Geography classroom was on the first floor above the English department. It was part of the new build as the old classrooms collapsed. Inside the classrooms it was a similar story. Pristine white walls surrounded a room that contained just the standard tables and chairs, with a teacher's desk at the front. Whilst some of the IT equipment was still being ordered, the teacher Mr. Artim was required to bring in his own laptop.

As the class settled Erik turned towards Adrian. It was the first time they had been together in class for weeks as they were placed in different temporary schools.

"So how was your replacement school?"

Adrian thought back to the time he spent at Carrick high school.

Carrick high school was a little bigger than Pittsburgh high school. They are one of the few schools to offer business technology and health technology programs. Their school was clearly more advanced than what Adrian was used to. Adrian knew this from day one. He arrived with a few of the other pupils he knew from Pittsburgh high school. He tagged along with them but ultimately he did not know them well enough. After a few days he separated from them and he was on his own. He would be the first to admit that his head was not focused on education. Since the incident and the questioning, Adrian's head was in several places. *What had he actually done? What does everyone think?* He also had to keep contact with Hannah after their date. That was the only positive though. Teachers noticed a slipping student more than a successful one. Adrian was that student. His lack of enthusiasm in lessons, inability to learn and communicate with other students sent alarm bells ringing for teachers from the first week.

It was in his Maths lesson that he was made aware of this. He had completed his homework over the weekend and handed it in at the start of the lesson. Half-way through the lesson the teacher Ms. Morris called Adrian outside. She handed him his homework complete with feedback. At the top of the sheet Adrian saw his mark. *Four out of twenty five*. Adrian had never gotten under fifty percent in anything.

Ms. Morris gave Adrian a solemn look. "Adrian. This isn't good enough. I need to see an improvement or I have no choice but to make the school and your parents aware of the situation."

Adrian did not know how to react. He was shocked in his own performance but he was also surprised at the ruthful attitude of Ms. Morris. But he offered no excuse. He stood in silence and stared up at Ms. Morris. A few tears began to trickle down his face.

"I don't want to upset you." Ms. Morris became more sincere.

"I'm sorry. I have to go for a walk."

Adrian escaped outside and walked a route around the high school. Ms. Morris was not aware of his personal situation. While she was aware he was involved in the incident at his own school, she did not know the extent of his involvement. All she saw were bad grades and a student struggling. It was not just the incident that was affecting him though. Adrian was in a new school and did not know anyone. None of the staff knew him and he did not feel he could confide in any of them. He was not settled. He felt the treatment from Ms. Morris was completely unfair. The fresh air outside helped him compose himself before he headed back to class. He walked in and took his seat. Some of the class watched him but most carried on with their work. Adrian just kept his head down and waited for the end of the day to come.

The next day Adrian stayed after class to have a word with Ms. Morris. He had been panicking the night before and spent considerable time trying to improve his homework. He made an improvement in the lesson, contributing more to the interactive aspects and showing more enthusiasm.

Ms Morris organised some papers on her desk before leaning on a table opposite Adrian. "Is everything okay? I think you've done a lot better today."

Adrian's glare circled the room before setting on his teacher. With a direct and measured voice he told her exactly what he was thinking. "I think you were a little unfair yesterday. To criticise me like that after you never gave me a chance… it's just… it wasn't right." Adrian's speech was stuttered but he was getting his words heard.

Ms Morris listened intently and smiled. "I think your right Adrian. I was a little harsh and I apologise for that."

Adrian was surprised by her response. "I don't understand... Why?"

Ms Morris inhaled. "Sometimes students need a wakeup call. Some of these students react badly, they continue to fail. The stronger ones though, they take it in. They improve. They prove me wrong. I think you're one of the strong ones Adrian."

Adrian nodded. His posture relaxed. "Thanks, that's good to hear but I don't think I'm anything special."

"I've had similar students, they don't do so well at the start but they've gotten good grades at the end and gone on to be very successful."

Whilst Adrian was flattered, he was a little annoyed. Adrian felt he was his own person. He did not like Ms. Morris trying to compare him to others. What this did do however, was make Adrian realise what motivated him. He seemed to respond well to criticism. Ms. Morris told him he was not good enough. He wanted to prove her wrong.

Adrian's mind jogged back into his Geography lesson, about to answer Erik's question.

"It was okay..." A solemn answer. "What about yours?"

"Same really, it was little more upmarket, hard to get used to!"

"Yeah true, the teachers seemed to expect a bit much."

Before they could say more to each other, Mr. Artim started the lesson. Adrian did not recognise him. *He **must be new**.* Whilst new teachers usually needed time to earn the respect of the class, Mr Artim's frightening nature instantly earned him the attention of the class. He scanned the class with his wide deep set eyes stopping at Adrian who became the centre of his focus. Mr Artim held his stare for what *seemed* like a few minutes. However, no one else in the class noticed except Adrian, who could only stare back at him. Adrian felt his body start to freeze up. Fear had taken over.

Empire

One Year Ago.

"Vision."

Sophia lowered her eyebrows. "What?"

"The guy at the end of the trailer. It's the Vision."

"Who's that?"

Theron sighed. "What are you a DC fan boy?"

In the depths of lower Manhattan stood the 13th precinct of the New York City Police Department. Sophia and Theron are detectives, colleting important data, searching for patterns and providing evidence to take down criminals. When they are working that is.

"I don't care that much for… heroes. I'm not five." Sophia turned back to her desk and shuffled her paperwork.

Theron placed his hand on his heart. "Ouch. You know you could hurt a lot of people saying that."

"I don't ca…" Sophia stopped mid-sentence. She had spotted a file Theron was holding by his side. "Isn't that for my investigation?"

Theron's eyes widened. He brought the file to the front of his eyes and pointed at it. "This one?"

Sophia nodded.

"Yeah, I was just getting verification from the team about how legit it really is."

"It looks pretty legit. Can I take a look?"

"You're the boss." Theron handed Sophia the file. She studied it carefully. The document's layout was synonymous with the largest drug trafficking organisation in the world, Sinaloa Cartel. Her speciality.

"Where did you get this?"

"It's a financial statement we managed to intercept."

"It looks exactly like something we would see from Sinaloa Cartel. But the details. The name, the address…" Sophia's voice lowered to a whisper. "They're different."

She quickly twisted towards her computer and searched the address. Her eyes lit up.

"It's a warehouse. One that's not on our database. This could be their New York base!" She dragged Theron down in excitement and made him stare at the screen.

But Theron was sceptical. "We can't jump to conclusions. We don't even know if this is real. It could be a set-up."

Sophia withdrew her feelings. He was right. But she was finding it hard to ignore her instinct. "But what if? We have the opportunity to take down one of the biggest criminal organisations of our century in our own backyard and we miss it."

Theron bit his lower lip and looked away in thought.

Sophia continued to reiterate her point. "The reason we struggle to catch these criminals is because we're too busy dealing with paperwork and 'verifying' our sources. We need to take risks."

Theron rubbed his chin as he considered what Sophia was saying. Then he nodded. "Okay, you take this to the chief. I'll make a few phone calls and see what I can do."

Sophia smiled and quickly gathered the paperwork to show her boss. But Theron looked concerned. He moved towards the exit, taking out his mobile phone and dialling his most recent contact.

"They've discovered your whereabouts. I'm not sure whether they will move in or not, but it's too risky. I would be unable to prevent it. You must evacuate immediately."

Theron watched Sophia raise her point to the chief. She looked happy. The attack was going ahead.

* * *

This was all his. His empire. A well-oiled money-making machine working like clockwork under his stewardship. Salazar was a proud man. Nothing said this more than seeing him break a smile as he peered onto the manufacturing floor below. But all good things had an end. Salazar crept into his office and rested his back on his high office chair, rocking and staring out the window. Things were not as smooth as they used to be. But nothing is perfect. Then he heard a slight knock on his open office door.

"Sir."

Salazar lowered his head and tilted it slightly to the left. The man spoke again.

"We've received a red alert from informer 238." The man hesitated. His voice was shaking. "We need to evacuate immediately."

Salazar sniggered. This could not be true. Even so, he was not threatened. They had enough firepower.

"We do nothing. Tell the frontline to alert me of any changes."

The man was shocked. "But sir…"

Salazar turned full circle and glared at the quivering man. "You have my orders."

The man knew Salazar had made a bad call. But arguing against him was not worth his life. "Yes sir." The man nodded and left the doorway.

Salazar was in no mood for an evacuation. He had too much work to get through. He had to search for a new financial advisor. And also find out what happened to the last one.

Gunfire. Explosions.

Salazar reached below his desk and pushed a sizeable black button. He calmly lifted himself out of his seat and stared out the window. He could see several troops emerging from the shadows towards the building. Simon lined up beside him.

"I know you don't want to hear this. But you must. There are too many. We're not going to win."

"Do you fear death Simon?"

"Sir…"

"Look at them. They put their lives on the line to protect us. You see the fear in their eyes. But they still go into battle. What else do they have?"

"With all due respect sir, I think you should skip to the point you're trying to make."

Salazar sniggered. "The police are inside. They have vacated the outside." A smile grew on his face as he peered at Simon. "Death may come next. We should not fear it."

Salazar grabbed Simon's shoulder and plunged both of them towards the ground below. The glass shattered on impact. They both landed on their sides, Salazar still clutching Simon around his shoulders. After a few moments, Salazar awoke. Still breathing. Simon was not. He had been knocked out on impact. Salazar rubbed his head and looked over to his unconscious assistant. He slid his arms underneath Simon's shoulders and dragged him out into the empty, quiet woods in the background. Salazar stopped around forty metres away from the warehouse. He could hear gunfire inside and his men falling to their deaths. There was nothing he could have done. The siege was inevitable. The gang had lost someone special. Their secret weapon.

Salazar observed his surroundings. Something felt strange. He sensed an importance to the area. He scooped up a small amount of soil from the ground. It felt fresh. Like it had been tampered with. The colour of it was not consistent with the rest of the area.

"Stop!"

Before Salazar could investigate, an armoured police officer stood above him, pointing a handgun at his chest. It was a white male officer. His eyes said he was inexperienced. His scars said otherwise. Salazar slowly lifted his hands in surrender and tried to inch away.

"Don't move."

"As you wish." Salazar smiled. "You can't kill me can you?"

The officer kept a straight face. "I don't have to. The gun is pointing at you, not me."

"But there is two of us. When he wakes up you're outnumbered."

"Something tells me he isn't waking up anytime soon."

"Still, you need to call for back up. If you're not going to shoot me then how are you going to stop me?" Salazar noticed a small drop of sweat roll down the officers agitated face.

"You need to be quiet or I will pull the trigger."

The officer tilted his chest and brought his radio up to his mouth. Salazar could not let him speak. He quickly rose to his feet but heard a gunshot. Salazar could not feel anything. He was shaken but not shot. The officer however, was clamouring for breath. His body started violently shaking. No longer able to stand, the officer fell to the floor into a pool of his own blood. Behind him stood a feminine figure.

"Looks like you missed me."

Salazar was a relieved man. "Ella, you're just in time. We need to get the hell out of here."

"We need to get Simon help."

"He'll be alright but we need to find somewhere else to hideout."

"I know a place."

Then the gunfire stopped. Silence engulfed the atmosphere. The fall of Salazar's empire was evident.

"Do you know if there are any survivors?" Salazar questioned.

Ella shook her head. "I don't think so. The police have fully taken over in there."

Salazar put his hand on Ella's shoulder. "I'm sorry about all this. I'm happy you're back."

Ella turned towards Salazar and smiled. "You've given me everything. You're the only person I trust now." She placed her hand into Salazar's palm and held tight. "Time will heal our wounds."

Trap Door

Adrian was finally feeling like himself again, at least on the outside. The rumours around the playground had stopped. His acts of courage were now ignored. Nobody took notice of him anymore but this was welcomed. On the inside though he was still feeling the after-effects. He had been suffering from transient insomnia caused by stress. Inevitably he could not focus in class or feel the need to work after school. It affected his social life too. He was short in conversations and started to become distant from his other friends and classmates. As quickly as it started he was no longer seeing Hannah. Their communication stuttered and finally stopped. Adrian did not want to expose her to what he was dealing with. It was better that he kept his distance from her although it did not make the decision any easier. In some ways it made it harder for him to deal with the stress. But as long as Hannah was safer it was a sacrifice he was willing to make.

It was a regular Wednesday at Pittsburgh high school and Adrian was in-between lessons. He had just left his IT class, a lesson he and Erik did not share. They would see each soon though, as they both had Maths next. With that in mind Adrian had to pick up his Maths textbook. He raced through the corridors so he could reach his locker before the lesson. As the locker came into Adrian's focus, he stopped abruptly. Glaring forwards he noticed the lock had been tampered with. He slowed his approach. The lock was broken, free for him to open the door. Adrian felt that same cold feeling he felt earlier as he peered inside his own locker. On top of his books lay a small piece of paper, slightly folded. He reached out and grabbed the small note. He unfolded it and read it. His heart skipped a beat. His whole body felt like it had sunk into the floor.

I know what you did

He flipped it over and noticed a combination of letters and numbers at the back.

SB 12

Adrian stared at the note for a minute. It was the room number for an old biology class in the science department. He glanced around to see if anybody was watching before crumpling the note up and stuffing it into his pocket. He grabbed his textbook, shut his locker door and moved on. Adrian walked into his Maths class with his head down, thoughts fixated on the note. He slumped into his seat next to Erik and slammed his bag onto the desk.

"Something wrong?" Erik innocently asked.

Adrian took a minute to compose himself. He turned to Erik and managed a wry smile. "Not really, everything's good."

Erik was amused by Adrian's sudden mood change. "I won't say anything then!"

The students were told to answer questions on a worksheet handed out by their teacher, Mr Church. As the lesson wore on, Adrian was becoming increasingly agitated. He was continuously checking his pocket and touching the note. His hands were shaking and he was making slow progress on the work. Erik could see Adrian was in some kind of distress. He was about to speak before Adrian shot his hand up and asked the teacher if he could go to the toilet. Mr Church nodded and Adrian left the room. *That's why*, Erik thought.

All the students were settled in their classrooms. The corridors were empty. Adrian was almost running through them. His nerves and built up energy was finally releasing itself. His pace reduced as he passed the toilets, but he did not stop. That was not where he was heading. He took the left turn at the end of the corridor and headed towards the science department. As he did the note slipped from his palm. Adrian approached the main double doors and entered the biology corridor. Now he was at walking pace. He could feel his heart beating through his chest. He had reached what students called 'the lost corridor'. It had been locked and never used for the entirety of Adrian's attendance at the school. Until now. The door to the corridor was now slightly open hung by only one hinge.

Adrian wondered through, careful not to break the door or make too much noise. The corridor had only two doors on the right, with a large window on the left. The light was shut out by the dust that had settled on the cage of the window. Both the doors on the right led to former

THE FRONT

classrooms. Adrian approached the first door. He wiped away the dust on the door label to see which room it was. **SB 12.** He cleaned away the dust from his finger and took a step back. His trembling hand gripped the spherical door knob. It was clean. Adrian took a deep breath and turned the handle. The door creaked open. As he peered inside all he could see was darkness. If he was to satisfy his curiosity, he literally had to wonder into the darkness. *The unknown.* He carried on giving the door a slight push until it was fully open. The light from the corridor only reached the floor in front of him. At the edge of that light he saw a footprint in the dust. Someone else was there.

Adrian carefully took his first steps into the room. He reached into his left pocket and picked out his phone using the flash on the camera as a torch. He scanned the room once over. There was some old tables and chairs stacked on the sides. The old blackboard was covered in thick dust as was the chalk. The model skeleton in the corner caught Adrian by surprise, until he realised it was a former biology classroom. The darkness started sweeping in. Adrian frantically turned around as the door behind him slammed shut. Now he was in complete darkness and he knew he was not alone. A loud voice echoed across the room.

"I'm glad you could make it."

Adrian's body froze. He could hear his heart pumping hard inside him. He desperately looked around for something he could attach the voice to. All he saw was darkness. Suddenly he felt a sharp pain at the back of his head. Within seconds Adrian fell to the floor. Now he was in complete darkness.

* * *

Mr Church was sat at his desk finishing up some marking for homework. He glanced at the class in front of him. A puzzled look grew on his face.

"Erik is Adrian not back?"

"No sir."

"Surly even a number two wouldn't take this long!"

The class giggled. Mr Church knew toilet humour almost always got them laughing.

"Will you go and check the toilets for me Erik."

"Okay sir." Erik lumbered out of his seat and walked out.

The toilets were located in the main building round the corner from the school's main meeting point, the forum. Erik passed the labyrinth of corridors and turned into the boy's toilet, not taking note of his surroundings. Inside there was no one. He shouted Adrian's name thinking he might be in one of the cubicles. No answer. He checked underneath the cubicle doors but he could see no one. With a sigh, he walked out.

He stood by the toilet entrance for a moment and looked around. Something caught his eye. He peered down and spotted a piece of folded up paper next to his foot. He leant down and picked it up. As he read the note he was caught in two minds. *Should I return to the classroom? Should I go and get Adrian myself?* He was not even sure if Adrian would be there. For all he knows this note could be completely unrelated. But Erik was suspicious, not least because this classroom had not been used in years. *Adrian could be up to something.* He would not bet against it. Erik took a deep breath and ran down the corridor.

I See Fire

The boy was unconscious. Anders used this time to tie the boy's hands behind his back and tie his feet together. He tried the classroom light but had no success. Luckily he had bought some candles and matches. He spread the candles around the two of them and lit them. He found an old cloth in his backpack and used it to cover the fire detector. He could not take any risks. From the same backpack he took out a petrol canister and poured it around the boy. After he circled the boy he swirled the petrol around in the canister and moved it closer to the boy's face. The fumes awoke Adrian. As his eyes stuttered open he gently lifted his head. Anders was staring directly at him, inches away from his face. Adrian shook his head to wake himself up. His eyes were fully open. He tried moving his arms but to no avail. They were stuck behind him. The friction of the rope was irritating his skin. Adrian glanced around the room, dimly lit by the candles. His focus returned to Anders.

"Mr Artim?"

Anders took this as an invite for an introduction. "You can call me Anders, Adrian. You know why you're here." Adrian took another look around the room.

"A romantic meal?" Adrian grinned.

Anders chuckled to himself for a moment. "Funny. You seem to show no remorse for the killing of my two friends."

Adrian continued to push Anders buttons. "Nice wife beater."

Anders was sporting a white vest and grey sweatpants. Adrian could see the candle light reflect of the sweat that had cumulated on his forearms. Anders grin suddenly turned more serious.

"Jokes over. Don't try and change the subject." Anders withdrew a large chef's knife from behind. His attempt to intimidate Adrian seemed to work. Adrian's mood swiftly changed. Now he had questions.

"Was it you that escaped that day?"

Anders ran his finger across the knife. "No, no one escaped. You either killed them or arrested them."

Adrian retaliated. "You threatened my friends!"

Anders voice grew louder and rougher. "Exactly, we didn't kill them! You on the other hand…"

"I don't regret what I did." Staring point blank at the knife, sweat started to roll down his face.

Anders was angered by Adrian's statement. He had to make a statement of his own. He had to show his intent.

"You know what I used to fear? I was seven, stuck in my room at night. I heard shouts from below. My mother was screaming, my father was begging for mercy. Then I heard footsteps climb up to my room. I hid below my bed. The man entered my room, his boots were in front of my face. Then he lowered himself."

Anders stood up and walked over to his backpack. He rummaged around inside it before pulling out a mask. Adrian could only see his back as he seemed to stretch the mask over his head. Anders continued his story.

"He peered into my eyes wearing this killer clown mask. He did nothing. But that image. That mask. Sticks in my mind. And do you know why? That day I walked through my house finding pieces of my dead parents. At the time I feared that mask. But then I realised, it was nothing."

Anders turned around revealing the full view of the killer clown mask he was wearing. The eyes were slightly drooped, with small red coloured tears hanging off the pupil. The centre of the pupils themselves were deep red, a colour which spread through the neighbouring veins. Blackness surrounded the deep set pair of eyes and the lips. The nose was a dark red deflated sphere. The teeth of the mask were long, white and sharp encompassing a large open mouth. They shaped out a sly smile. The red fluffy hair was split into three parts. Each as messy and long as the other. The rest of the mask was cream with darker patches and ridges near the forehead to simulate a real face.

Surprisingly Adrian was unnerved. "That's a great story but I think you've underestimated me."

Anders moved towards Adrian holding the knife close to his chest.

"Don't get smart with me kid!"

Anders was now inches away from Adrian. He bought the knife up to within millimetres of Adrian's neck. He softly ran the knife across drawing drops of blood. Adrian held his breath in pain.

Anders whispered gently in Adrian's ear. "Give me a good reason why I shouldn't just kill you right now."

* * *

Erik had returned to his Math's class, stopping at the doorway. The door had been kept open and he could not see Mr Church. He turned to one of the students at the front of the classroom, Curt.

"Where is Mr Church?"

Curt stopped writing and glanced up. "He went somewhere with Mr Walker."

"Where? Why?" Erik's speech was frantic and short.

"I think I heard Mr Walker talking about the new English teacher. Something about his paper records."

As Curt finished his sentence Mr Church brushed past Erik and stood at the front of the classroom.

"Attention class. I feel you should all know that I have been reliably informed that your English teacher Mr Artim is not who he says he is. I don't want you to be alarmed but any of you see Mr Artim please let the nearest member of staff know as soon as possible."

He then turned to a stunned Erik who was still at the doorway.

"Did you find Adrian?"

"No sir, but I think I know where he is. I think I know where Mr Artim is as well." He handed Mr Church the note. "I also think we will need back up."

Mr Church gazed at the note. "Erik, you cannot join us."

"What?"

"This school has a responsibility to protect its students. Mr Artim could be armed and dangerous."

"If that's the case then surely the school should have been evacuated by now!"

Mr Church sighed. "You can't come with us Erik. Now step aside we're wasting time."

"Adrian's my friend. I am going with you!"

I SEE FIRE

The teachers shared a look. They both nodded to each other and turned back to Erik.

"Fine but you have to stay at a safe distance behind us."

"Fair," Erik replied.

Mr Church and Mr Walker led the way, joined by the school police officer Clancy. They crept through the empty corridors, reflecting the journey Adrian had taken just moments ago. They arrived at the darkened Biology corridor and turned into the 'lost' corridor. Both the teachers waited at either side of the room **SB 12**. Erik stopped and waited by the Biology corridor. He managed to get a small view of the action from a crack in the corridor window. Officer Clancy faced the door. He held out his gun and pointed it downwards. He glanced at both the teachers and nodded. In one movement he raised his leg and stomped his foot on the door, smashing it open. He entered the classroom and held his gun up.

"Freeze!"

He was faced with no one. In front of him was an open window where the sunshine beamed through. He followed the light until he saw a student strapped to a chair on the side. Adrian's arms were locked behind him, his mouth covered in tape. He was making sounds but none of it could be understood. He started using his head to point to the window. Officer Clancy quickly ran over to Adrian and removed the tape from his mouth.

"He escaped through the window!" Adrian shouted.

The two teachers entered the room and attended to Adrian untying his hands and inspecting the cut on his neck. Officer Clancy ran to the window and peered outside. He could see no one.

"I don't see him."

"Let me go I can get him!" Adrian blurted. He was desperate to leave his seat and give chase.

Mr Church remained calm as he held Adrian back in the seat. "I'm sorry Adrian that's not happening, you need to come with us and rest."

"I will go and look." Officer Clancy drifted through the window.

Giving up, Adrian sat back in his seat and looked up to the heavens.

High Hopes

Adrian stared down at his ticking watch. The black stainless steel strap wrapped around his bruised wrist. The watch face was a simple silver dial with white lines as indicators for the numbers. With no second hand, Adrian could only watch the minute hand tick along. He was sat in Mr Church's head of Maths office. It was one of the more narrow rooms in the school. In front of him was a wide desk and empty space. In the centre of Mr Church's desk was his school standard computer, out-dated but it got the job done. Beside his computer Adrian could see a photograph of what he was assuming was Mr Church and his wife together on holiday. He also saw what seemed like a collection of artefacts resembling the Aztec culture. Adrian was always curious to find out the significance of objects teachers kept with them.

Mr Church entered the room through the door behind Adrian carrying a pile of paperwork. He placed the paperwork on his desk and sat down in his office swivel chair, rolling it over to small table where Adrian was.

"So, what was that all about?"

Mr Church was a young and tall character. He had a calm but inviting presence often giving away a professional feeling but as the staff and students knew, he would regularly go outside of this. Mr Church was wearing a dark navy suit that was almost black. His shirt was a light blue and his tie was black with a cluttered white polka dot pattern formed. He placed his blazer on the back of his chair and turned his focus to Adrian.

"Why did the school hire a monster?" Adrian was swift and direct with his response. He felt the school should shoulder the blame.

Mr Church thought the best way to deal with Adrian would be answer his questions first. "He passed all the screening necessary to become a teacher here. Eventually we found him out and just in time. You were lucky."

Adrian offered no response. Instead he raised the ice pack he was holding in his hand and put it onto his neck, the cut still visible.

HIGH HOPES

Mr Church leaned forward in his chair. "After all you have been through Adrian, the school has managed to shield you from any police questioning. All they ask is for me to ask you a few questions so we can establish exactly what happened."

Adrian looked away from Mr Church. "What are those things on your desk sir?"

Mr Church looked back at the Aztec antiques Adrian was pointing at. "I got them from my holiday in Mexico a couple of years ago."

"Is that… is that a dog?" Adrian's voiced his first thought at the artefact on the far left.

It was a long object, made of brown wood and covered in ancient patterns. At the front was the face of an animal Adrian interpreted as a dog. It had two paws pushed forward beside the face painted with black nails.

"It's actually a musical instrument. We call it a Teponaztli Drum. It originated from the Aztec era. The two sticks next to it are the drum sticks."

"What about the disc next to it?" Adrian saw a large silver plated disc covered in similar Aztec patterns.

In the centre was a face with what looked like an upset expression. Around this were four main arrows pointing in each direction; North, South, East and West. In between these were smaller arrows. Each 'row' of the circle was separated into different patterns and symbols.

"That's the Mayan calendar. The Mayan's were an intelligent tribe. They used their own interpretation of time and events to create this. They believed at the end of the calendar, which was actually this year, significant change would happen in the world."

"The end of the world?" Adrian questioned, familiar with the popular culture at the time.

"Not quite the apocalypse as it is widely interpreted but rather the end of an era and the start of a new one."

"But nothing happened."

Mr Church rolled his eyes and sighed. "Yes, well… that's one thing they didn't get right. So, what can you tell me about what happened to you in that room Adrian?"

THE FRONT

With Adrian talking more freely and engaged, Mr Church felt this was the right time to change the subject and get what he needed from Adrian.

"It started with that note I found…" Mr Church listened, nodded and took notes as Adrian continued to briefly describe what happened to him. He revealed Mr Artim's real name and detailed their conversation. A few minutes later he reached the end of his description.

"… He was about to slit my throat when he heard you coming. Then he just vanished through the window."

Mr Church finished making his notes. He started to realise this was bigger than he imagined. Widening his eyes, he delved deeper into Adrian's thoughts.

"Adrian, do you think this was linked to the previous attempted robbery at the school?"

"Of course, there isn't any other explanations."

Mr Church noted it down. "Since this doesn't appear to be an isolated incident the school will be stepping up its security to keep you safe. Are you happy with that?"

"Whatever is necessary I suppose." Adrian was not bothered by any measures the school took. If anybody was after him, he knew they would find a way.

"Before I let you go, there is something else. In light of the circumstances I know this is difficult. I have just graded your Unit 2 test for Maths."

Adrian looked up with concern towards his teacher. He knew this was going to be more bad news.

"Adrian, you got eight out of forty. I am sure you're going to be disappointed with that. So are we."

Adrian had a sense of deja-vu. Mr Church gave Adrian a sympathetic look.

He continued, "I don't know whether it is personal issues, but I know, you know and everyone knows you are capable of a lot more than this. Being successful starts here. I want you to think about that."

Adrian quietly replied. "Yes sir."

He stood up and turned away to the door, glancing at Mr Church whilst doing so. Adrian had a lot to think about.

HIGH HOPES

* * *

Roberto Salazar sat back in his high, thick padded black chair. In one hand he held a cigarette. He was addicted. In the other a mobile phone against his ear. In front of him was a large bottle of Red Label whisky and small glass on top of a large wooden table. The room was only lit by the small halo of light coming from the doorway opposite. Outside, shouting and screaming could be heard. Salazar lifted his glass of whisky off the table. He held it for a moment, swirling it in his hand and listening to the man on the other end of the phone. Suddenly his mood changed. The glass stopped swirling in his hand. Without warning Salazar sent it hurtling towards the wall. The glass smashed and began to rain down onto the floor. Whisky dribbled down the wall in streams. With his typical dominant and angry tone he spoke the first word.

"WHAT?"

The voice on the other end now seemed ten times smaller. A nervous gulp was followed by confirmation Salazar did not want to hear. Confirmation delivered in a tense tone of voice.

"He's dead sir."

After hearing the final word Salazar slammed his mobile phone onto the desk in front of him. Both of his elbows were on top of the desk as he sunk his head into his hands. He held the position for a minute before finally lifting his head up. He grasped the handle of a drawer to his right and forced the drawer open with an almighty pull using the anger built up inside him. After reaching into the drawer and rummaging through several bits of paperwork, he pulled out a small business card. The card was blue, with a picture of the globe in the bottom right hand corner. On the left, contact details were listed:

LUCAS ARKWRIGHT
TRINITY CORP.
TEL NO: 412-778-0714
"INVEST IN A STRONGER TOMORROW"

Salazar stared at the card for a few minutes deep in thought. He picked up his mobile and dialled the number. It was time to call an old friend.

THE FRONT

Once Salazar had finished with the phone call, he stood up and slowly made his way over to the door. Stood in the hallway, he was staring out onto a large house. Either side of him were curved stairs leading down to the sitting room. As the centre of the house was open plan, he could see down to the sitting room himself. The house was not empty. People were continually going inside and outside the front door at the far end of Salazar's view. That though, was not the centre of his view. Instead he stared at the women sprayed across the house. Dressed in only their underwear, they were dragging men towards their bedroom's using their ties. The men in the sitting room just had to wait their turn. Not Salazar though. He had his favourite.

"19 GET OVER HERE! I need some release."

Salazar's voice echoed across the house and managed to get everybody's attention. A slim brunette women quickly shuffled towards him. She was wearing matching black underwear and suspenders. The bra was a thin sheet of silk that could be seen through but the underpants hid her secret with the help of thin strings that ran from the top to halfway down. She looked like she was in her early twenties and her skin tone was white but slightly tanned. She wrapped her arm around Salazar's and took him to the room next door. She closed the door behind him.

It had been another tough day on the job.

Champion

Just one more turn and then a straight finish.

Mrs Leones' heart was pumping fast. She could feel her body tiring with every step. It she was to improve she knew she had to deal with the pain. She had to fight the urge to stop and keep going. She got closer, pushed harder and tightened her focus as she approached her house. Now she was within reach. She just had to pass two more houses.

Her pace slowed down. She felt a sense of accomplishment overcome her. She closed her eyes and reflected over her own personal accomplishment. Upon opening her eyes, however, she was faced with reality. She was heading for a man in a large red coat holding a large rucksack in one hand and a pile of letters in the other. She tried to stop but he was too close. She collided with the man knocking the letters out of his hand. They both managed to keep their balance and stay up.

An apologetic Mrs Leones started catching her breath. "I am so sorry Mr Peterson."

She quickly got to her knees and picked up the letters sprawled across the street.

Mr Peterson shook his head and helped Mrs Leones back up. "That's quite all right. You need to watch where you're going!"

Mrs Leones laughed along. "I'm sorry, I really do apologise."

Mr Peterson got hold of a few letters and handed them over to Mrs Leones. "I believe these are yours."

Mrs Leones thanked the postman and headed inside her house. She started flipping through the letters as she closed the door behind her. She noticed the last one was from Pittsburgh High School. She placed the others on the counter next to the door and ripped through the top of the letter. She unfolded the piece of paper inside and had a quick read through the main points. It was Adrian's term report. On the whole, he had done quite well but at the bottom Mr Church had highlighted Adrian's latest bad grade as a possible slipping point. Mrs Leones was disappointed.

"Oh Adrian." She quickly muttered to herself. She stood holding the letter in her hand and spared some time for thought. Finally she decided to call Adrian down.

Adrian was taking the day off, allowed by the school, to recover from any stress or anxiety. He had just got out of the shower and dried himself off when he heard his mum shouting him from downstairs. He grabbed some blue chino shorts from his wardrobe and pulled on a white polo shirt from a hanger. With a quick spray of deodorant he left his room and made his way down the stairs. The open-plan layout of the house saw Adrian immediately confronted by his mother in the sitting area at the foot of the stairs. He could see her wearing her running clothes. The pink tank top could be spotted from a mile away and she had finished the outfit off with half-length running tights and purple running trainers with Nike branding.

"Got your report from school." Mrs Leones waved around the letter in the air as Adrian reached the bottom of the stairs.

"Room for improvement?" She questioned.

Adrian stared at the letter. "Sorry."

"Adrian, there is no need to apologise. Come here."

Adrian stepped closer to his mother as she passed him the report. She put her right arm around him, stretching to his shoulder.

"I know it's tough. But it's your time to show the world how special you are. That is what your father wanted. Not this."

Adrian looked up, curious. "What do you mean?"

"Your father saved up some of his money especially to send you to college."

Adrian raised his eyebrows. "What?"

Mrs Leones nodded. "He really believed in you Adrian. We both have enormous faith in you."

"Thanks for the pressure." Adrian grinned.

"We know you can handle it or I wouldn't say this to you!"

Adrian nodded. "I'll try my best."

He disappeared back into his room closing his bedroom door. He pulled out a notepad from the chest of drawers adjacent to him and grabbed a pen. Settling down on his bed, he opened the notepad to the first blank page. Then he started to write.

CHAMPION

30/01/2013

8/40. This grade hurts. I don't care what I've been through. What I have suffered with. I should be doing better. Sometimes, life kicks you down. Kicks you down so hard that you just can't get up. All you can do is lift your arms and crawl to the finishing line. Who cares, you still get there in the end. Except, it's not the start or the end of the journey that's important. It's the journey itself that's important. Do I really want to crawl the whole way having started so well? I'm not content with that. No one should be content with that. I want to rise, I want to stand up and be counted. Then I'm going to sprint past that finishing line. But I just realised, that my biggest strength will also be my biggest challenge. Myself.

- Adrian

Strangely, the latest threat to Adrian's life had spurred him on. He seemed more determined than ever to be successful. At least for his father and his mother. In recognising that he can improve, he also realised that handling himself could be the challenge he was not expecting. Adrian closed his notebook and placed it back inside his drawer in the far corner where it could not be seen in plain sight. He sat down at his desk and positioned his failed exam paper in front of him. With almost unhuman focus he took in every dropped mark and made a note of his mistakes. From now on, Adrian was ignoring any distractions.

Goodbye, Apathy

New Pittsburgh Research Facility. Suitably dressed in a grey suit, a man approached the large facility situated on the outskirts of Pittsburgh. Upon arriving at the main entrance, he positioned his eye to the right and stared directly into a scanner. Red lines searched his retina before returning its verdict.

"Welcome Mr Stone."

The door opened and he was now faced with a large reception area. The floor and furnishing all glowed a shiny white. The main reception desk to his right looked like an elongated sphere had risen from the ground. It was finished with a company logo in the centre, TRINITY CORP. backlit by a glowing light blue colour. The man continued his journey, passing reception to the elevators near the back.

This facility was the home to Trinity Corp. They were an organisation founded by two brothers, the Williams brothers. Trinity became the number one provider of medicine to Eastern America almost a decade ago. Today, they produced a turnover of around six hundred million dollars and a net profit of around four hundred million dollars in just a single year.

The Williams brothers were committed to using this money to continue development in medicine. They funded research into finding cures for conditions such as; Alzheimer's, Cancer and HIV/AIDS. They not only provided funds to other organisations but invested heavily in their own research facility, now known as the New Pittsburgh Research Facility, guaranteeing work for local graduates. The facility stretched to around fifty thousand square feet. It was split between different departments which were run by their own project leaders. Trinity was now an efficient and well-oiled machine so there was no need for the Williams brothers to visit too often. Instead they worked on building international relations and looked into ways to expand their growing empire.

The man was faced with the elevator panel. Rather than selecting a floor though, he entered a special code into the number pad beside the buttons.

Once his code had been accepted a small fingerprint scanner popped out of the number pad. He placed his finger on top of the panel and the scanner lit up green. His finger was valid. The elevator then began to drop. He looked up at the LED screen displaying the floor number, watching the elevator get lower and lower; *-1... -2... -3...* Finally, the elevator stopped at the negative tenth floor.

There was one special project the Williams brothers wanted to work on. With the resources and the staff at hand, they could finally deliver. After a lengthy recruitment and screening process they personally selected a team of twelve consisting of some of the greatest minds in Biology and their team leader, Lucas Arkwright. Lucas was a close friend of the Williams brothers growing up. They all shared the same dream and aspirations to be rich, different and better. He was a friendly, intelligent and diligent character. This was the main reason the Williams brothers decided to recruit him in this position of power. Lucas was around when they first started their business but decided not to take a share in ownership and follow a different career path. When the Williams brothers approached him about the opportunity he was working as a Stock Broker. Initially it was hard to convince him to leave. He was earning a lot of money and was considering settling down with his family. However, this project was his dream. He finally had the chance to do something different with his life. In the end he took the chance.

One hundred and eleven feet below sea level the elevator doors opened. What the man was staring at was top secret and only known to the thirteen team members and the Williams brothers. One of those team members had just arrived for work. Lucas was the first and only person to greet him. He stood on a small ladder wearing a long white lab coat, with a blue checked shirt underneath. He was holding a screwdriver and working on an electricity unit.

Lucas looked longingly at the man before smiling. "Malcolm Stone or should I say detective! Welcome back! It's good to see you."

Malcolm walked over to Lucas. "It's good to see you again!"

"How did they treat you in the police?"

"Well. It was good fun. How's the project coming along?"

"A lot better than before you left! That information you gave us was vital. Now we can start trials. Let me show you."

Lucas climbed down from the small ladder and walked over to the main part of the large open room. The roof extended to forty feet above their heads. In the centre were five identical swivel chairs, all close to their corresponding control panels. The control panels were almost a square meter in size and curved around the space creating a circle encapsulating the main research area. Opposite to each control panel, Malcolm could see high blocks tilted backwards, all interconnected with twisted wiring. All four blocks were covered with a grey curtain. Behind him, there were two rectangular windows both at different points and heights, where scientists could be seen at remote control panels and discussion areas. They were clearly safety rooms built with thick glass at a safe distance from any activity.

Lucas emerged from a small area right of the centre, separated by an arched way. "What we're doing here Malcolm, its special. We couldn't have done it without you."

Lucas moved over to the first block on the far right. He grasped the side of the cover and pulled it back. Malcolm's eyes grew large. He was rendered speechless by what he was seeing. With the first one unveiled Lucas moved onto the other block until all four were in clear view. Lucas stood by Malcolm's side putting his arm around his shoulder and smiling.

"It's shocking when you first see it. But our dreams are finally coming true." Lucas gazed at the sight of glory ahead of him. "Please excuse me for a while. I have a friend to show this to."

Lucas left Malcolm to stare, still speechless. He got into the elevator and disappeared. He arrived at the ground floor and glanced around. The night had just closed in. He could see the darkness through the glass walls. There was a large man waiting for him at reception. Lucas started walking towards the reception desk to collect his visitor but stopped abruptly. He narrowed his eyes and took a closer look outside. He could sense an uneasy presence. Lucas attentively continued his walk towards his visitor.

"Ah Salazar, long time no see!" Lucas greeted Salazar with a handshake.

Salazar seemed flustered. Lucas was not looking at him however, he was looking over his shoulder. Far into the distance he saw an unfamiliar small light in movement. He choose to ignore it and carry on his conversation.

"Lucas, we have a lot to discuss." Salazar replied.

"Please, follow me down to my office, I have something to show you."

Salazar was wearing a dark navy suit with a red shirt, black tie and red handkerchief in his blazer pocket. Lucas and Salazar made their way down to Luca's special project headquarters. As the elevator reached the bottom, Lucas offered a small warning.

"It may not be easy on the eye, so don't take too many steps forward."

Salazar lowered his eyebrows. Now he was curious.

The door gently opened. Salazar took one step forward and his eyebrows instantly raised. Ahead of him, Salazar could see unconscious humans, strapped to what looked like tilted concrete blocks. He could see four of them, two men and two women. Attached to them were transparent wires fixed into their necks, wrists, ankles and hips. Through the wires he could see a red liquid flowing, with small breaks as it flowed into the humans. Each block was controlled by a single wire connected to its corresponding control unit in the centre of the room. All the wires were interconnected with each other, flowing between different blocks, stopping at the ends.

"Human trials are the best part of my job!" Lucas stated. "I apologise, I have not introduced you both. Salazar, this is Malcolm Stone, one of the researchers working on this project. Malcolm did some undercover work for us at the police. Malcolm, this is Salazar a member of Sinaloa Cartel and a close friend."

Salazar gave away a slight smile but he was not comfortable around an ex-cop. He turned back to the centre of the room.

"What is this all about?"

Lucas grinned like he was going to enjoy the answer. "This is our vision for the next stage of human evolution."

This raised more questions than answers for Salazar. "I don't understand."

"Imagine you could harness pure energy from a single element, without the need of a generator per say." Salazar was still confused.

Lucas took them both into his side office and sat them down. He offered drinks but there were no takers. Sitting back in his chair he continued to explain himself.

"What we do is quite simple. We turn the blood into the generator. Then when we add our chosen element, we have walking energy. With power beyond human imagination."

"Has this actually worked?" Salazar asked.

Lucas responded with a chuckle.

"Not yet. You see, the humans we tried before, they were not strong enough. They collapsed and became weaker. So we decided to find stronger people. You see, some people are just born to be stronger than others. Its evolution. We want to give these people extraordinary abilities."

"Where did you find these people?"

"That's where Malcolm came in." Lucas nodded in Malcolm's direction. "We knew the government authorities were hiding accounts about these special people. They would track them from a young age. Malcolm went in and sent us their information."

"What, then you just go and kidnap them?"

Lucas looked concerned. "What other option did we have?"

Salazar looked on astonished at what he was hearing. Then a wry smile grew on his face.

"I like your style." Salazar's smile grew bigger.

"Excuse me, but how do you two know each other?" Malcolm finally decided to have a say in the conversation. He knew the orders were strict on allowing personnel to the underground base.

"Good question Malcolm." Lucas nodded to Salazar as a gesture for taking the question.

"We did some business together quite a few years ago now. I got involved in the drugs trade with his gang. With my chemistry knowledge, I helped them turnover quite large profits selling some of the finest stuff on the market."

Malcolm was surprised. "Drug dealer to stock broker, that's quite the jump. How did you manage that?"

Lucas nervously laughed. He looked at Salazar and put on a straight face.

"I was actually never a stock broker."

Malcolm's expression turned to anger. "You mean you lied to everyone."

"You would not have my expertise if I was not here. This project would be dead in the water. I lied for the sake of humanity. They wouldn't have hired me if they knew I was dealing drugs. The Williams brothers are good, honest people."

"So, what is he doing here then?" Malcolm rolled his eyes towards Salazar.

"I have the same question Malcolm." Lucas looked at Salazar.

Salazar stared back at them. He rested his posture and calmly responded to their concerns. "You mentioned this special project and your dealings with stronger people before. I have a little situation at the moment. Someone is killing members of my team. I know it's bizarre but I believe he may be… what you call more evolved. You were the only one I knew would have the technology to deal with him. But I see now you need him."

"Well at the moment we don't need him."

"But you will."

Lucas held that thought for a moment. Malcolm stayed quiet. He did not know Salazar's business and he did not know the status of the project enough to comment on that either.

"If we are successful, he will become stronger than what he already is. What makes you think this will be a good idea?"

"If that happens we will be the least of his problems. He would have served his sentence in my eyes."

"How is he serving a sentence?"

Salazar struggled to keep his smile away. "No matter what happens to him, he will never be the same Adrian again. That, for me, will help me sleep at night."

"Wait, did you just say Adrian?" Malcolm edged his way back into the conversation.

"Yes, do you know him?" Salazar looked surprised.

"I interviewed him about the explosion at his school a few months ago. Wait… it was your gang wasn't it?"

"Yes, he caused severe damage that day."

Malcolm felt outraged. "He's a sly kid but he's not evil. You can't just murder him in cold blood!"

Salazar gave Malcolm a sinister look. "With all due respect Mr Stone, this is none of your business."

"I'm working on this project!" Malcolm turned to Lucas. "Lucas, I am not here to kidnap children and commit murder."

Lucas strayed onto the side of caution. He stayed quiet and listened to what each of them had to say. But he had a decision to make. All eyes were trained on him.

Lucas took another moment to reflect.

"I think before any definite decision is made, we should wait and see what happens with the current trials."

"You can't seriously co – "

Malcolm was cut short by a loud smash echoing across the room. All three men watched the centre circle as a large stone hammer smacked onto the floor. Several bits of heavy glass followed it with a thundering noise.

Then silence.

Everyone in the room looked at one another. Lucas stood up and began to shout instructions towards his team.

"Call security, someone has infiltrated base." His face grew with rage. "I WANT THEM CAUGHT!"

Crazy Love

One Year and Six Months Later. Exam Time. Adrian was facing his final exam season before he moved to college. In the past year and a half he had gone from strength to strength. His hard work and natural ability put his scores at the top of his class and the good grades just kept on coming. Now it was show time. His chance and in some ways his final chance, to prove he is capable of further education and fulfil his father's wishes. He had already chosen his desired college. After a mini-tour of New York, Adrian decided he wanted to go to Columbia University and study Maths. Maths had become Adrian's strongest subject and most enjoyable. With his future decided he could focus on making sure he made it.

He had worked hard for the past few weeks to give himself the best chance of performing well in the exam. Much to the disappointment of Erik. Whilst he was happy Adrian was finally in his element, he wished he would try and be more social. Outside of school, Erik had not seen Adrian for three weeks and even in school he would not be distracted from class. Being a good friend, Erik left him alone. He remembered it was a chance for him to work hard himself. *Maybe it is for the better. We can hang out after exams.* Erik was also curious to find out the background to the events Adrian was involved in. However, Adrian consistently brushed it off and insisted he was not involved in anything. Adrian was confident these incidents were over and that Mr Artim would not be back. Erik had to believe him, after all, a year and half had passed without incident.

Adrian was stood outside the exam hall, alongside his other classmates. They were about to sit their first exam, Maths. Adrian was slightly nervous although he tried not to show it. He stayed calm, revising the content in his head. Erik just arrived and saw Adrian standing alone.

"Hey Adrian, are you ready?" Adrian looked up and smiled.

"I think I am, how are you feeling?"

"Quietly confident." Erik followed up with a small laugh. Adrian quickly took a serious mood.

THE FRONT

"I'm sorry I haven't made much time for you recently. My grades were slipping and things were playing on my mind..."

"Adrian, its fine, I get it. I think it's given us both a chance to get our heads down."

Adrian agreed. An invigilator emerged from the exam hall. She shouted above the students to get their attention and then proceeded to read out some instructions.

"Students must leave their bags and coats at the side of the exam hall or at the front. Once you are at your desk you cannot take off your coat without the permission of an invigilator. You are only allowed water, stationary and tissues on your desk. Your mobile phones should be switched off and placed in your bag."

Adrian and Erik both checked the seating plan and then entered the exam hall. It was a large hall filled with columns of desks. Each column had around a hundred rows of seating. The invigilators stood at the front beside a large whiteboard and below a large clock. Adrian first found his seat, around twenty rows from the back. He put down his stationary items and clear bottle of water before placing his bag at the side and returning to his seat. He filled in the boxes at the front of the exam paper and then kicked back in his seat and relaxed. The invigilators ran through some more instructions before then turning to the clock and waiting for right time to begin. Adrian started to feel the adrenaline building. He was eager to get started and start writing some answers down. Everyone was fixated on the large clock. The outstretched second hand ticked closer to twelve. Then the words all the students longed to hear.

"You may begin."

The ruffle of papers greeted the start of the exam. Adrian was just as quick as the others. He first took a couple of minutes to read the questions and decide the order he was going to answer them in. He took a deep breath and proceeded to open his answer paper. He picked up his pen and pressed it against the paper. Nothing. He sat and stared at the blank page looking back at him. He was searching his brain for answers but it returned nothing. Adrian froze. Staying calm, he took another deep breath. A couple more minutes had passed. He was tempted to look around and see how the other students were coping. But he had to focus on himself. After taking another look at the question paper, the answers, methods and numbers started to hit him. He grabbed his pen and began to write.

Adrian had finished. The exam still had around ten minutes to run but most students had put down their pen, checking and double checking their answer paper. Adrian could not bring himself to look over what he had written. He was probably more inclined to make small mistakes than most students but still he chose not to check his answers.

"Please stop writing." The invigilators sounded the end of the exam.

Each student drew a breath, slouched into their seats and relaxed. They held out their answer papers ready for collection and were then dismissed column by column. When it was his time Adrian collected his stationary, grabbed his bag and headed outside. *One down five to go.* Erik waited for Adrian outside the exam hall and navigated his way through to talk to him.

"How did you find it?"

"It was okay. I don't wanna say much until I get the results! You?" Adrian never wanted to sound too confident, he felt he would just set himself up to be knocked down.

"Yeah I thought it was okay. Onto the next one now! Let me guess, you're gonna go home and revise."

Adrian smiled. "You know me too well."

The two friends then headed in separate directions.

* * *

Adrian submerged his face into a pool of water keeping his eyes closed. After a few seconds he lifted himself back up and rubbed his hands over his face. He stared at himself in the mirror. Today was results day. All the hard work completed in the past couple of months came down to this one day. His summer had been quite relaxing. He kept his promise of spending time with Erik after exams. Erik now had a full driver's licence so they both took a road trip to Cleveland and spent the day by the lakes. Adrian knew he had to treasure moments like that, since they won't see each other often once they start College. He was not even sure if they would stay friends. Contact between old friends becomes limited if they do not see each other regularly and eventually the friendship dies out.

Adrian had also met up with Hannah again. He felt he needed to apologise and make things up to her so they shared lunch. They both enjoyed each other's company just as friends, sharing laughs and making jokes about the moments they spent together. They acknowledged they had both learnt a lot since their time together. They wished each other good luck for the future and then separated. But they did see each other again. Adrian and all his classmates attended their class of twenty fourteen prom. Handsomely dressed in a slick black suit and dinner jacket, Adrian took the hand of a gorgeously fashioned and classy looking Hannah. Together on the dance floor they shared a slow dance to Michael Bublé's rendition of 'Crazy Love'. By the end of the song Hannah put her open lips on Adrian's and they shared their last kiss.

Those were moments Adrian would never forget. Today though, was about making sure he could make similar moments in his future. College was a chance for him to start again. He wanted to start fulfilling the potential he has always been told he had. Adrian was sat alone in his room staring at his computer screen. His results would be released at ten in the morning and he would be able to view them on his school account online. *10 minutes to go.* Nervously, Adrian checked his account early but they had not been published. Next to him, his phone started vibrating. It was Erik.

"Hey, you still waiting?" Adrian asked.

"Yes are you? I am getting pretty nervous."

"Yeah me too. Good luck man, stay on the line."

"Yeah sure, good luck to you too."

After a tense few minutes of silence, Adrian was alerted to an email. "Hold on, I've gotten an email from Columbia Uni."

He felt the adrenaline pump through his body. This could be a welcome email or a sympathy one. He opened his email account and glanced at the subject line.

"I don't believe it!" Adrian's voice filled with excitement. He was on the edge of his seat.

"What is it?" Erik sounded excited too.

"I've been accepted! I'm in!" Adrian's face was now fixed in a permanent smile. He clenched his fists and punched the air.

"Congratulations Adrian, you deserve it! Hang on the results have been published!" Erik's voice was trembling. Adrian calmed himself down and became nervous again for his friend.

"How did you do?" Adrian dared to ask.

"One second…" They both held a breath before finally…

"Yes! I've done it!" Erik's voice filled with the same excitement Adrian felt. They were both now screaming, laughing and punching the air sharing a mobile phone high five in the process.

"I need to go and tell my mum!" Adrian shrieked.

"Me too!"

Adrian ran downstairs to his mum in the kitchen. He was jumping for joy and screaming. His mother thought he had gone mad. *It must be good news if he is having this much fun.* But she soon realised that he had gotten his results and started celebrating alongside him with similar elation.

Both Erik and Adrian had reached their desired destinations.

The start to the rest of their life had just begun.

Madness

"Are you taking that?" Mrs Leones asked pointing at Adrian's tennis racquet. It was a Wilson 2011 Rodger Federer edition, coated in white and red paint and bearing the famous players name along the side.

"Yes" Adrian replied.

"Are you going to take up tennis?" Mrs Leones questioned with a growing smile.

Adrian shifted his eyes side to side. Then he looked at his mum. "Maybe…"

His mother laughed. She was helping him pack all of his University gear into the car ready for the trip to New York later in the day. Adrian was nervous. He had never been independent before and being left in a flat with strangers to live with was not his idea of fun. But he had to learn to live on his own. Adrian watched as the last of his paraphernalia entered the car.

"That's it. Are you ready?" Mrs Leones shut the boot of the car.

Adrian stood by the passenger seat. His face and body was frozen.

"Adrian?" Mrs Leones said his name again to get his attention. She looked slightly concerned.

Adrian shook his head, like he had just re-entered real life. "Sorry, I spaced out for a second."

"Are you ready?" Mrs Leones asked again with a softer tone.

"Not really, but I have to do it." Adrian smiled. His mother's concern soon turned to confidence.

They both jumped into the car with the same edgy anticipation. Mrs Leones began the journey from Adrian's home town to Columbia University, New York. As they got closer Adrian could feel his nerves but more importantly he started to feel excitement. Adrian pulled his phone out. Mrs Leones looked to her right, curious. They passed a sign directing the traffic towards New York City and Adrian snapped a picture of it. He knew his mother was watching.

"What?" He looked at his mother hoping to hear what she was thinking.

"Nothing." Mrs Leones just smiled and carried on driving, her eyes fixed on the road. She could tell Adrian was starting to get excited and she could not be happier for him.

* * *

Facing the large accommodation blocks Adrian felt like he was undergoing an out of body experience. Seeing the campus in front of him made it all real. He told his mother to stay with the car whilst he collected the keys from the centre building. Once he returned they both made their way to Adrian's accommodation block to find his room. Whilst walking through the flat they passed some people. Adrian did not know if he was passing his new flatmates, their siblings or the current students helping out. He could not take in his surroundings. He wanted to get to his room, build base and take everything from there. Adrian and his mother reached his room at the far end of the flat. Adrian held the key, took a deep breath and opened the door. Adrian's new bedroom was an en-suite room consisting of a desk, wardrobe, bed and bathroom. Adrian and his mother took turns to unload the car and fill his room. It was almost full when a tall male student identified by a brightly coloured blue t-shirt appeared through his door.

"Hey guys, how are you doing?"

"We're okay thanks." Mrs Leones was quicker to respond.

"That's great. Just to fill you in on what's happening today, once the parents leave we'll gather the flat into the kitchen to give everyone a chance to get to know each other. Then tonight we'll have a speech by our college provost and some free pizzas." Mrs Leones looked at Adrian and raised her eyebrows.

"I'll let you get on with unpacking but if you need anything just give me a shout."

"Thanks." Adrian was the first to respond this time.

The student left and Adrian turned to his mother. "I'm the one that is supposed to do the talking you know."

"Sorry, mother's instinct." Mrs Leones laughed. Adrian kept a straight face.

THE FRONT

The time for his mother's leaving was drawing nearer. They placed the final boxes out of the car and into his room. His mother made his bed and stocked up his fridge and freezer in the kitchen area. Adrian moved around his room changing small details to make the room more personal. He placed a set of holiday souvenirs on the window ledge, set up his laptop and speakers and hung his solar system poster up on the wall next to his bed. The latter was a gift from Hannah, the only memory from home he had taken to university. He and his mother then gathered together in his room to say their final goodbyes for the next few months.

"Well, I should be getting back now." Mrs Leones' tone took a sad tone.

This moment was going to be the most difficult for Adrian, despite all the excitement he was feeling. He and his mother had grown a lot closer since his father had gone missing and he felt it was a situation they got through by being together. Now they both had to face a future without reliance on the other.

Adrian stayed speechless. His mother offered him a hug. "Stay safe okay. Make some new friends. Don't worry about me."

"I'll come down to the car with you." Adrian kept a neutral expression.

They both reached the car and hugged for the final time.

"Bye Adrian, I hope you have lots of fun."

"Bye mum, look after yourself."

Mrs Leones climbed into her car and they waved goodbye as she drove away. All of sudden Adrian was free.

Adrian returned to his new room and continued unpacking. He still had to organise his clothes and some office equipment stashed in a box by the window. As he trudged over he heard a voice by the doorway.

"Hi, everyone is gathering in the kitchen if you want to join us."

"Sure." Adrian followed the brunette to the kitchen. He could not help but think she looked like Hannah from the back. After coming through the kitchen doors he was faced with five other apprehensive faces sat near each other at the round kitchen table. The kitchen area was large, split into two parts. One side had worktops, ovens and cupboards. The other half consisted of one round table as a general seating area. Adrian took his seat at the chair closest to him. After a few seconds the brunette girl introduced herself.

"Hi everyone I'm Sophie and I'm actually a New Yorker myself. I think we should go around the room and introduce ourselves."

To Sophie's right there was Gemma from Stockholm followed by Jayden, Crystal and Antony. Then last but not least Adrian.

The group seemed genuine. On the face of it they were kind people although naturally a little reserved at first. They discussed their hometown, results and why they chose Columbia University. Each student was in the same situation. Living away from home for the first time and with complete strangers. How the students reacted to the new environment changed with their personalities and attitudes. Adrian wanted to turn the people around him from strangers to friends.

In the next few days Adrian became closer with Sophie, Antony and Jayden. Sophie had a down-to-earth and friendly character which helped Adrian feel at ease around her. She was studying Biology and came from a higher class family. Antony was Adrian's closest friend. He was on the same course as Adrian so they had more time to get to know each other. They were similar in personality and background. He was quiet but once he got to know someone he would become a pleasant person to be around. Jayden shared the same taste in comedy as Adrian. He did not take anything too seriously, a trait developed from having two brothers. He had come to New York to study Aerospace Engineering, leaving behind a quite popular following in his hometown. Jayden completed the social group of the flat.

Once Adrian had a spare moment he drew out his diary and made the first entry of his new life.

11/10/2014

First day – Well, the day finally arrived. My life in the boot of the car transferred to New York. Then the final goodbye to my mother and I was overcome by the feeling of freedom. Half unpacked and door stop in use Sophie poked her head around my door 'we're in the kitchen.' The phrase I always use to describe my neighbour Sophie for the first few days was 'free spirit!' I met all my flatmates, terrible with names at first. For me, it was drinking games and bed. Drinking games... welcome to University. Oh and free pizza at the centre building. The reps arranged a secret night out but only a few went, not including me.

- Adrian

Strangers

After a few weeks Adrian knew who his friends would be. The other two flatmates, Crystal and Gemma decided to make their own friends so he did not see them often. None of the group knew why they did not make an effort. In the end they were just different people. They stayed strangers to Adrian but it did not matter. Adrian was relishing the time away from home and appreciating his close friends. At home Adrian had memories he never liked to go back to. Here it was a new start and a chance to grow through independence.

He had spoken to his mother a few times since watching her leave on move-in day. It was always a simple "everything's fine" conversation but it was priceless for Adrian to hear a familiar voice again. He had been messaging Erik too. They were both getting used to college life together so they found their home comforts in one another. It took Adrian about seven weeks to shake off any unease and become fully immersed in the experience. He had been cooking, washing and had some really good nights with his new friends.

Adrian and Antony were at one of their Maths lectures. In the past week they had started to talk to a couple of other students on the course, Alexa and Jack. They met Adrian and Antony during a group activity in a practical and soon started going to lectures together. Adrian had struggled to adjust to lecture-style teaching. He could only keep his concentration for fifteen minutes before he lost his focus and lost understanding.

A distracted Adrian turned to Antony. "Who do you think the lecturer looks like?" He whispered.

Antony quietly laughed at his question. He turned towards the lecturer and thought for a moment.

"Have you seen that show Rules of Engagement?" Antony replied.

Adrian leaned closer. "Go on…"

"He looks like that Russell character." Antony continued to laugh with Adrian now joining in.

"That's what I was thinking, it's uncanny."

Alexa and Jack were sat beside Adrian and Antony. They heard them both laugh and wanted to learn more.

"What are you guys talking about?"

Adrian turned to Jack. "We just noticed the lecturer looks like Russell off Rules of Engagement."

"I haven't seen it." Jack responded.

Adrian stopped laughing and dropped his shoulders. He reached into his pocket and pulled out his phone.

"That guy."

Jack stared at Adrian's phone and started a stuttering laugh.

"Let me see that." Alexa wanted to see what they were all laughing about. She stretched out to Adrian to reach his phone. After a minute of glancing at his phone and the lecturer she started giggling quietly to herself.

She placed her hand on Antony's upper arm, still giggling. Antony eyes opened wider as he turned to Adrian, sending a confused facial expression in his direction. Adrian responded with a shrug of his shoulders.

Alexa passed the phone back to Adrian. "That's a pretty good spot."

"What do you guys want to do after this?" Adrian opened the question to everyone in the group.

Alexa was the first with a suggestion. "We could get some lunch from one of the student bars."

Alexa had moved closer Antony to make sure her voice was heard. Antony was starting to feel uncomfortable.

Adrian was enthused. "Great plan. What's that place called near the big white place?"

"You mean the college's centre building? I think it's called the Boulevard?"

"Does everyone wanna go there after?"

The group agreed and carried on listening to the lecture.

Afterwards the four students made their way across campus to The Boulevard student bar. It was recently refurbished establishment, built and run by the independent student union for use by students. Adrian and his friends entered through the main entrance. The bar had a soft and cosy feel with the use of wooden features and spongy sofas. Adrian spotted a couple of large HDTV's hung on the wall, one at each end. On the right of the entrance, a small set of stairs led to the bar and a few tables. On the left was the main seating area which extended outside with a couple of large glass doors. The bar had a few groups of students inside but it was not busy. The group found a table and passed around the menu to see what they wanted to order. Adrian was the first to go the bar and make his order. He returned with a pint and a food order number. Once Antony, Alexa and Jack had made their orders they settled into a conversation.

Jack was the first to talk. "So how's everyone finding the university so far?"

Adrian was the first to reply. "I think it's been good. I love campus and the course seems okay. What do you think?"

"The campus is really nice. I like my flat too."

"I hate my flat!" Antony replied looking at Adrian and sharing a laugh. Jack and Alexa stared at them both with confused expressions.

Adrian felt he had to explain. "We're actually in the same flat."

"Ohhhhh." Jack and Alexa responded in unison. "What are your flatmates like then? Any fun?"

Antony answered. "There are a couple we don't see much. But the others are pretty cool. What about yours?"

Jack offered his response. "We hang out sometimes but mostly they're just in the rooms. It gets kinda boring."

"I think my flat is good. There are a few girls so it's easy to socialise. But I think I do need guy mates around!" Alexa added.

"Glad you have us then?!" Antony joked.

Alexa smiled back. "I suppose." She continuing staring at Antony.

"Where are you all from?" Jack asked, changing the subject.

"Pittsburgh." Adrian replied.

"What's it like there?"

"Like any other city really. Some nice restaurants and a few lakes."

Alexa zoned back into the conversation. "I'm a capital girl. Washington DC. It's always busy! But it's a nice place to live. What was school like?"

"Mine was pretty average, few were decent people. Most aren't at college now though!" Jack replied.

Antony agreed. "Yeah same here. Some of the teachers were shocking."

"How so?" Adrian was curious.

"Well... it didn't seem like they cared. They spent all their time with the underachievers. Learning was purely based on getting grades."

"It's like that in a lot of places nowadays."

"True." The group nodded in agreement.

"Did you all hear about that school in Pittsburgh that got robbed at gunpoint?" Antony's tone suddenly turned excited. Adrian inched back in his seat.

"That wasn't your school was it Adrian?" Alexa asked.

"No no, I went to... to... Carrick high school." Adrian replied. He wanted to change the subject quickly. "So has anyone been into the big city yet?"

"Once, I think it will take the whole three years to properly explore it!" Jack answered.

At that moment one of the bar staff approached and brought two dishes of food. He placed them in front of Alexa and Adrian.

"What did you get?" Alexa asked.

"Cheeseburger and chips. It's looking good too. You?"

"Chicken wings and stuffed peppers. Smells lovely."

"That sounds interesting." They both smiled.

The staff member returned with Jack and Antony's food.

The group stayed silent for a moment whilst they started eating their food. Adrian broke the silence, talking about their upcoming deadlines. They continued their conversation until they had all finished eating. They left the bar together and stood outside.

"Well, I'm gonna go back to my flat now, they wanna go shopping!" Alexa left the group and headed in another direction. Jack stayed with Antony and Adrian for a moment until he had to go another way to his flat.

"It's been good meeting up with you guys. We should do this more often."

Antony and Adrian were left to walk back to their flat.

"What do you think of them?" Adrian asked.

"Nice people, some Maths students can be pretty nerdy but those seem pretty cool."

"Yeah definitely."

"And that Alexa…"

"What about her?" Adrian raised his eyebrows and turned to his friend.

"Adrian she is stunning. I think… I'm in love."

Adrian began to laugh. "Seriously?" He responded.

"Do you not think?"

"Yeah she is good looking but I don't have feelings for her!"

"I just feel this weird thing around her."

"Okay, now you're creeping me out!"

Antony started laughing along. It sounded better in his head.

"I don't know mate. Let's see how it goes…" Antony sounded confident.

Adrian shook his head. University was just beginning.

Fear

Pittsburgh was being hammered by rain. All the residents had taken shelter inside their homes. The sun had set and the darkness of the late evening had taken over. Most people had finished work. Security guard Mike however had just started his night-shift at the New Pittsburgh Research Facility. One hundred feet below him lay the unconscious bodies of two men and two women. That was about to change. Second from the left, a man's eyes flickered. His hands moved slightly. His fingers began to expand and contract. The man opened and closed his eyes continuously for a few minutes.

Until they opened permanently.

He felt like his heart was going to rip out of his chest as his heartbeat increased. He frantically moved his head side to side. The man had no idea where he was. He looked down at his own body and saw wires flowing into his bloodstream. His muscles tensed. His eyes widened. His fists clenched. With a mighty pull the metal straps around his wrist collapsed. His eyes turned hot red. The man ripped out the wires one by one, spraying blood across the room each time. But the man felt no pain.

Large red LED lights surrounding the room began to light up and the speakers echoed a warning message across the entire building. The man knew he had to escape. With every passing second he felt more powerful. The energy started to build up. The man started to sink into the ground. The concrete beneath him crumbled. The energy was released in less than a second. The man went crashing upwards into the roof of the secret basement. He found himself in mid-air above the main part of the research facility but, falling unconscious, he dropped back down to the ground.

Security guard Mike was inside the CCTV office. Hearing the loud crash he rushed to the epicentre of the incident. The buildings emergency alarms were sounding all around him. He withdrew a gun from his holster as he approached. As he got closer he saw a man lay on the ground. His head was tilted downwards towards his arms which were flat and bent at the elbow. His legs were flat and slightly twisted. His eyes were closed and he was not breathing. Mike hurried down to him and checked the pulse on his neck.

Nothing.

Mike tipped the man onto his back and separated his arms and legs. He placed both his hands onto his chest to try and resuscitate him.

Nothing.

Mike's eyes were fixated on the man's chest as he opened his eyes. The man lifted his back, stood up and gazed down at the stunned security guard. He then picked the guard up by his neck. Mike was staring directly into the man's deep red eyes. The colour was so deep it appeared to be leaking from his pupils.

Mike felt fear.

Fear coursed through his body.

The man smashed Mike into the far wall. Mike instantly fell to the ground on impact. He only had one breath left. But all he could do was watch the man fly through the ceiling and disappear.

* * *

Lucas was awoken from a deep sleep. His mobile phone next to him was buzzing with activity. He had installed his own alarm to alert him to any emergency at work. He was paranoid about anybody touching the project. People thought he was crazy. Now though, it was paying off. He grabbed the first clothes he saw, jumped into his car and headed down to the research facility. Lucas knew it was vital he got there ahead of the police. If they found out what was happening underground there would be outrage. The project would be finished and everyone working on it would be arrested. His life would be over.

As the facility loomed all he saw was emptiness. The rain was still pouring down but there were no police in sight. He entered the building to silence. The door to the security room had been left wide open. Nobody was inside. Lucas ran to the elevator and dropped down to his department. He looked towards the blocks. *Shit.* He glanced at the roof and noticed the large hole. He had some serious questions. He quickly climbed back to the ground floor and made his way to the cancer research department, where he saw the large hole once more. At the side he saw the security guard injured and concussed.

"What happened?"

The guard was struggling to get his bearings. "A man... red eye... he... *flew.*"

"Did you call the police?"

"No." The guard fell unconscious.

Lucas was relived. He pulled out his phone and called all the scientists and senior staff including the Williams brothers.

This is a problem.

Lucas only had to wait ten minutes before the first workers arrived. It felt longer. Two scientists pulled up in the same car and spoke to Lucas. The team quickly established that the status of the other humans had to be checked first. Lucas decided he should check the location of the escaped trial. Each human had been fitted with a GPS locater for any emergencies. They were attached inside the neck to ensure they could not be removed. Lucas jumped onto a computer at reception and opened the tracking software. Nothing. The tracking software could not pick up the GPS signal.

Luckily Lucas had another plan. By emitting a small radio wave he could manually track the GPS. He grabbed his specialist radio and started sneaking around the building to detect the signal. As soon as he turned it on he heard a faint noise. *Surely the human did not stay here?* He followed the signal as it got louder. He passed the cancer research department, the signal still becoming an increasing noise. Then, in the corner of his eye, he spotted a small blinking LED light. His radio now became a constant pitch of noise. He picked up the small device and confirmed it was the GPS tracker. *How did they get rid of this?* Lucas made his way to the front of the facility again. Most of the scientists had now arrived. He ordered them to cover up the hole in the ceiling and the floor to ensure their project was kept confidential. Outside, he could see a smart silver Bentley pull up. The Williams brothers were here.

The Williams brothers were African-American and dark in skin colour. They both wore black suits with white shirts. One of them wore a red tie and the other a blue tie, with Trinity Corp gracing the side of each. They strutted inside the building and looked at Lucas from head to toe. Lucas' hands began to tremble. Even though they used to be friends, they were the kind of people that did not give anybody second chance's. Lucas wanted this to work out.

"What is happening?" The brother on the left spoke. His voice was deep and he had a New Yorker accent.

Lucas was staggered in his response. "One of the humans for the trials has escaped."

The Williams brothers looked at each other before turning back to Lucas. Their threatening eyes continued to unnerve Lucas.

"I can ensure you this is the first of these problems we have encountered in the year and half we have been running this."

Once again the Williams brothers looked at each other. They were not convinced but there was something else on their mind.

"You have been running trials for a year and a half?" The other brother spoke. He had a similar tone to his brother but with a lighter accent.

"Yes…" Lucas could guess what was coming next.

"You have made no progress in the past year and a half?"

"You have to understand we're trying. I know we're close to a breakthrough. We just have a little problem."

"Do you understand how much investment we have put into this project? Our time is not cheap Mr Arkwright."

"I understand but what we're dealing with… we haven't finished studying it yet. We don't understand how it works. The people we can use for this is limited."

"Are you saying you cannot use this on normal people yet?"

Lucas stared into the brothers eyes. He suddenly felt ten times smaller. He had no response. At just the right time for him bright lights and siren noises illuminated the night ahead of him. Two police officers stepped out their cars and knocked on the glass pane.

"Let us in please." One of the officers yelled.

Lucas hurried over to the large door, entered a code and opened the door. The police officers came inside and looked at Lucas and the Williams brothers.

"We received some reports of a loud noise here a while ago. What… What are you all doing here? What's going on?" The police officer scratched his head as he glanced around and awaited an answer.

Lucas decided to take the question. "We… are checking in on the facility. Our alarms were sounding."

The police officer opened his arms and shrugged. "Well… What did you find?"

Lucas took a few seconds to respond. "I think we were robbed."

"Robbed…? Why didn't you tell us straight away?"

"I was going to review security footage and consult with the Williams's security team here."

"Where did you get robbed?" Lucas pointed to the doors at the far end. "We'll have to take any footage back to the station to investigate?"

"It turns out the footage was removed. This thief must have been good. He knocked our security guy out cold."

Lucas led the police officers to the Cancer Research department. He was praying the scientists had finished covering up the hole in the floor. Lucas opened the door. The lights were still on but nobody was inside. There was a noticeable patch on the floor.

"This is the Cancer Research department. As you can see the robber entered through a giant hole in the ceiling. He must have blown it open and set our alarms off."

"What's that patch on the floor?"

"Ah, I think there was a spillage the other day. From what I heard the chemicals eroded the floor and the builders have patched it up temporarily."

"Do you want us to get an ambulance for that guy?" One of the officers spotted the unconscious Mike in the corner.

Lucas had forgotten about the guard. "Oh yes please. He still has a pulse, I was just about to call an ambulance."

"Radio we need an emergency ambulance to the New Pittsburgh Research Facility ASAP."

"Rodger that."

"So is this your department? Where you work?"

"No… no I work in a… different one."

Before the officers could question Lucas further they received an emergency call on their radios.

"All units we have dangerous situation developing on Beacon Street. All units must go to Beacon Street ASAP."

"Rodger that."

"We're sorry but we have to go. We have to investigate this properly so we will be back. I'll make a note of it."

Lucas exhaled in relief. "Thank you sir. Have a good night."

The officers disappeared back into their car and switched on their sirens. Lucas joined the Williams brothers again. He decided to raise his concerns with them.

"That police call could be our problem…"

"How so…? They said dangerous."

"That's exactly what we're creating." Lucas replied.

* * *

Lucas and three other scientists arrived at the scene on Beacon Street. The surrounding streets had been blocked off and a few people had emerged from their houses to see what was happening. Lucas and his team decided to keep their distance. They could not risk the police seeing them if this was caused by them. Through the gaps they could see the police all pointing their guns at just one target.

"Surrender yourself now," one police officer yelled.

Lucas decided to get a better view of the target by leaving his team behind. Then, in the distance, he saw him.

The red eyes.

He could see vehicles on the street that had been overturned and scattered. *Surely he is not capable?* Lucas dared to ask the question. As he watched on the man lifted his head up to the sky and screamed. The scream reverberated through dozens of square miles. Everyone in the proximity covered their ears. Then his eyes lit brighter. The colour extended to metres in front of him like two focused lasers.

The man fell to his knees. The light started to appear through his face as it cracked up. The man yelled again. His body was breaking up. His skin was being torn apart from the inside. The soaring heat was tearing through him. It was now so bright nobody could stare directly at him. Then a shockwave pulsated through the streets. Everyone within a three mile radius felt a small earthquake.

Calm.

Lucas turned back as the darkness drew in once more. He saw the police surround what was left on the floor. All they could see was ash. All Lucas could see was ash. The man had incinerated from the inside. Burned alive.

Nirvana

Antony was in love. He had never felt this way about anyone before. He was a changed man around Alexa.

Antony came from a quiet town near Boston. Like Adrian, his school life was ordinary. Except he did not have criminals to deal with. His intelligence allowed him to achieve similar grades and enrol at Columbia University. Antony dated a girl for a few months in the year coming up to college but this was just a relationship to satisfy his curiosity. The feelings he had now felt real. It was unconditional. He did not have to think about it to know it was there. Antony was not sure if Alexa felt the same way. He knew girls could sometimes give off mixed signals. They will get close to you, hug you and even sometimes kiss you. But it could all be because you are just friends. A friend that they trust. He wanted to become someone Alexa trusted. That would require time.

Antony was sat in a small study area of the Maths building. Adjacent to him were a row of seats behind a table that was up against the wall. All the seats were empty and nobody was in the room. Antony was trying to answer some questions for their end of week assessment. But he found himself procrastinating more than working. Behind him, he heard a voice calling for him.

"Antony I didn't know you were here!"

Antony looked back to see Alexa's locks of chestnut-brown hair wave across her glowing, porcelain-like skin. Straight-nose, full lips – she seemed the picture of perfection. Antony stopped for a moment, speechless. All he could do was smile. She approached him and sat on a chair nearby. She placed her bag on the table and turned to Antony.

"Do you have any plans for tonight?"

Just as Alexa asked the question, Antony felt his phone vibrate. He lifted it out of his pocket and looked at it. It was a message from Adrian.

"Hey man, do you wanna meet up and watch the game tonight? I was thinking Boulevard..?"

Antony turned back to Alexa.

"What did you have in mind?" He asked her.

"Well, I was thinking you and Adrian could come round to my flat, have a few drinks with the girls and if you want, go out."

"That sounds great. Can I check with Adrian first?"

"Sure."

Antony asked Adrian if instead they could go to Alexa's flat and hang out with her friends. Adrian was reluctant at first but in the end he succumbed and agreed to go along. This ended up being the first time of many that Antony decided to bring Adrian along to events with Alexa. To Adrian it was obvious what he was doing. Eventually, Adrian got tired of constantly spending time with them and decided to stay with his flat.

Finally there came a time when Antony and Alexa were on their own. Alexa told Antony she was bored and most of her friends were busy. She asked him if he wanted to meet up for a drink in the sun. Antony felt this was his chance to tell her the truth. He met her outside the Boulevard. She looked stunning as ever. Again, all Antony could do was smile. He enjoyed these moments, even if they did just end up being friends. But that was not enough for Antony.

They ordered a drink inside and then grabbed a table outside in the spring sunshine.

"Thanks for coming here. I thought it would be a waste not to get a drink in this sunshine."

"Yeah..." Antony smiled along.

"Did you go home the other weekend?"

"Yeah, it was nice. It's helpful to get out of this environment."

"I get it. Some things can just drive you crazy. How is your little sister?"

"She's okay. I think she misses me!" Antony chuckled.

"Aww bless her." Alexa's voice was soft and caring.

"So what are you thinking about doing after University?"

"Wherever the wind takes me!" They both started laughing. "Seriously I am not sure. I'd like the opportunity of a stable job in finance afterwards and then who knows. What about you?"

"I'm sort of on the same page, it will be nice to get some money after college. But there has to be more to life don't you think?"

"Of course, everyone has dreams. What's yours?"

Antony's hand began to tremble. She may have just set him up for the perfect moment for him to say something. His heart pumped harder.

His voice trembled. "I would love… to be one of those serious Maths professors one day."

Alexa smiled at him. "What's stopping you then?"

Antony relaxed back into his chair. "Well… I don't think I'm good enough for it. Who am I to come up with new ideas and make a difference?"

Alexa looked at Antony with sympathetic eyes. She offered some advice that Antony would never forget.

"Maybe because you want it so much, you think you're not good enough for it."

Antony looked at his hands on the table and thought for a moment.

"Maybe you're right."

Antony felt like all his problems had been solved. Every issue had disappeared. All he could do was smile at her. It was exactly how Antony felt. He knew he did not have the courage to tell her now. The moment was perfect. It just was not going to happen.

That afternoon lingered on Antony's mind for the rest of the week. This love had been spiralling around in his mind. He wanted to know what Alexa thought of him but another part of him did not want to know. Antony could not deal with his thoughts anymore. He had to tell someone. Better yet he could write it down. Antony grabbed a refill pad by his desk and ripped an A4 page out. He picked up his pen and let his thoughts out on the page.

Alexa,

I've realised that I have feelings for you. They've been there since the start of last term. I just had to be sure. I have tried to fight them, to let them go, but they won't go. It's hit boiling point. I created the perfect opportunity last week. I took you to the quiet place and a drink at the Boulevard but I chickened out.

You remember we were both talking about our dreams and how I wanted to do research but didn't think I was good enough. You said something to me 'Maybe because you want it so much, you think you're not good enough for it.' Well that's how I feel. You mean a lot to me, but fear of rejection limits my words.

All the time I spend with you, I feel lucky. I treasure each moment.

- Antony

Once he penned the final sentence, Antony dropped his pen, folded up the piece of paper and placed it amongst several items in his draw. If he ever found the right moment. If he ever needed to find the right words to say, he knew where they were. Antony realised he had not spoken to Adrian in a while. He picked his phone up from the desk and sent him a text. Adrian's reply was short and uninterested. Antony wondered if this was having a negative effect on Adrian too. Antony had not shared his feelings with anyone. After his first conversation with Adrian he did not want to talk about it more. It was his problem after all. Who actually cared?

Antony glanced around his room and stared at some of the posters on his wall. By his bed he had a picture of him with his close family. His little sister had been his shining light. She will always be the girl he would always have the time for. He saw his Dad, reliable and caring. He had been everything you would want in a father. He had an honest job and he protected his children in the best way he could. His mother was not there. She had passed away from cancer a few years back. His father struggled to cope as his work suffered. But with Antony's help he managed to overcome the grievance. It still hurt. It was damage that would take time to repair. In many ways, Antony saw his mother through his little sister's twinkling eyes. In his mother's memory, Antony helped the Williams brothers open their new facility in Pittsburgh. He became one of the ambassadors, whose story would promote the positive effect their research could have.

It took a lot of courage for Antony to move away to University. He would much rather spend time with his family and help them through their life. His father though, told him he should go. Antony had to begin his life. He had to make sure he lived his life properly just like his mother would have wanted. As Antony sat in his bed and continued to stare up at the poster, he started shedding tears.

Being in love is the best feeling in the world. But it can also be the most painful part of life. Even though you only want the best in your life, without the worst there is no life. There is no best part. Being at University was enabling Antony to experience life. His first love. His trip to Nirvana.

Runaway

The graphic images were etched on his brain. Lucas could not forget the moment he watched Patient 31 shed flesh and blood over the streets of Pittsburgh. Then watched as he imploded. It seemed like one failure too much for Lucas. He had tried to make his dream come true. It just was not working. They had made too many sacrifices. Lucas and his team had failed to perfect the formula. It was something they had to accept. The authorities will be asking questions. Lucas needed to know what he was going to do next. The project risked full closure and arrests would be made if they find the other Patients. There was no way they were going to make any breakthroughs soon. It was all over.

With Lucas' position of power, he would be responsible for its failures. But he feared another problem. He would be liable for all the kidnappings and murders. There was no way out.

He had to get away. Soon.

But where? Where could he actively find shelter from the police? To be with people that knew him and avoided the authorities as a job. *Salazar.* That was the answer. He had not seen Salazar in a year. They had been in close contact but Salazar had decided Adrian was no longer a target. By being involved in Lucas' project, the teenager could cause more damage to his gang. There was no guarantee the sample would kill him or whether they could stop him if it did work. *Malcolm's words must have got to Salazar.* The teenager had been quiet recently. But Lucas knew Salazar would ultimately want his revenge. There was not a better time than the present and Lucas had a secret weapon.

He stared at Salazar's phone number on his mobile. He tapped the green phone and it started ringing.

"Yes." The voice on the other end was stern and direct. He sounded like he did not want to be bothered.

"Salazar, the project… it's not working. The police are sniffing around and it's not safe for me to stay here."

Lucas heard a sigh on the other end.

"If you come here, then you put us at risk. They're not looking for us."

"Don't kid yourself. They're always looking for you. I'm offering you the chance for another member Salazar. One with my knowledge."

"What value is your knowledge to this organisation?"

"I have something special that nobody has seen. It's quite special I assure you."

"What is it?"

"You can only truly appreciate it when you see it with your own eyes."

The line fell silent.

"Meet at 5th street corner in two hours."

The line went dead. Lucas slipped his mobile back into his pocket and frantically circled the room. He grabbed a suitcase and stashed some clothes inside. *What about Malcolm?* Lucas did not hesitate to ditch the other scientists but he needed someone else with him. Malcolm deserved a chance. Lucas pulled out his mobile once again and called Malcolm.

"Malcolm listen, the project is dead in the water. I'm getting away."

"Wait what?"

"The escaped patient last night, it's exposed the project. Soon the authorities will link the two and they'll put us away Malcolm!" Lucas was sounding more frantic by the second.

Malcolm chose to stay calm. "So what are you going to do? Where are you going to go?"

"I've been in touch with Salazar, I'm meeting him at 5th street corner in about two hours."

"You know I can't be with that group. They're evil."

"Malcolm listen! I think I know who was responsible for all this. They can help us get justice!"

"Can you not wait? Get some sleep, you're not thinking straight!"

"I wish I could Malcolm. But their investigations don't rest. Soon the whole team will be tracked. Including you. It's now or never Malcolm."

Malcolm stayed quiet. Time seemed to stop still for a few moments whilst Lucas awaited his reply.

"I'll see you there." Malcolm hung the phone up.

Lucas began to drag his suitcase towards his front door. As he was about to open the door, he heard a knock on the other side. Hesitant, Lucas peered through the eye-view on his door. It was one of the scientists, Rebecca. He opened the door. Rebecca was about to speak when she saw Lucas' suitcase.

"Where are you going?" She asked.

"Rebecca, now isn't a great time."

"I can see that. I was just at the facility with the other scientists. Police have evacuated and cornered it off."

"They're already there? What did they say?"

"They said they're investigating a robbery. We all know that wasn't the case." Rebecca grinned. "So why the suitcase?"

"If the police find the basement, then we're done. You understand that? I'm getting away from here. What are you doing here?"

"Well, I came to see what you were going to do about all this. But I think I know the answer. You know that special extra 'project' we have going on is still down there."

"Yes I know. We need it. I promised a friend."

"I hope it's a friend. That is deadly in the wrong hands."

"Right now I'm willing to take that gamble."

"So how are you going to get hold of it? The police are swarming the place."

"Believe it or not, there is another entrance."

* * *

Rebecca had been dragged back to the research facility where she had been working for the past two years. She initially joined as part of the emergency disease response unit. The owners though felt she was better placed in this special project because of her breadth of knowledge. The special project was failing quite badly. It needed fresh ideas. Unfortunately she could not fulfil that duty. Not only was she uncomfortable with the work, she could not see a way in which the outlined goals could be achieved. Quite simply, it was science fiction. She did start to work with Lucas on something different however. She had noticed the power intake of using Patient's whole bodies was unnecessary. Using a big sample simply proved too much.

Rebecca and Lucas worked on a device that injected small doses of the formula into the wrist. Not only was the device more portable, but it could also be practical. They experimented with methods to attach Graphene on top of it, to create what was essentially a smart watch. Lucas was desperate to recover the prototype. Since Rebecca had worked so hard on the device, she did not want to see it in the wrong hands. Especially considering how dangerous it could be. She considered whether she may actually see it being used. *Not without someone exploding.* They were about a mile off the facility, in the middle of an empty and grassy field.

"You remember when we had that intruder about a year and a half ago?" Lucas began.

Rebecca sighed. "Yeah, all he did was throw some stuff around. We never heard anything since."

"Yeah well he managed to create a whole new entrance himself." Lucas pointed to a small hatch about a meter from Rebecca. They both knelt down next to it.

Lucas turned the handle on the hatch and opened the door.

"Are you saying one guy did this? That's impossible."

"It could have been more people. But think about it. We know there are people out there capable of this. We have been working on them! We know their biology."

"Are you saying that one of those guys did it? How would they know about what we're doing?"

"That I don't know. And the fact we've heard nothing recently suggests it shouldn't be a cause for concern. But I do have one theory. Remember I was talking about my friend, Salazar?"

Rebecca could not help but blurt out his name uncontrollably. "Salazar!"

"You know him?"

"What?"

Lucas repeated the question. "Do you know him?"

"No, its... it's just a funny name. Go on..." Lucas gave Rebecca a funny look as she moved some hair behind her ear.

"Apparently someone of this... strength has been after him and his friends. I think this guy may have been following Salazar on the day of the intrusion."

"Wow that seems like a reasonable assumption."

"If I go to him then finally, we can find out the truth. Try and track this guy down and have our justice." Lucas sounded like he had gone crazy.

"Justice?"

"Whatever this guy did it doomed the project from day one."

Rebecca decided to talk some sense into the scientist. "Lucas, stop looking for someone to blame. This project was doomed the moment someone thought it up."

Lucas sighed. Rebecca was right. "I still need somewhere to hide out. So do you. Do you wanna join me?"

"I suppose I don't have a choice if the police are going to come after me."

"First thing is first, let's get the Grapheos."

Lucas jumped onto a small ladder leading down the hatch. Rebecca followed him down. The small tunnel was pitch black and made Rebecca feel claustrophobic. The more they descended down the less light they could see from the already murky air.

The tunnel also had a lack of a pleasant odour. It seemed it had been built to intersect with the sewerage system. Lucas and Rebecca both reached the bottom of the vertical tunnel. They were faced with a large path and a straight direction. Below them were small puddles of dirty water. Rebecca lifted her shirt above her nose and mouth. The temperature had dropped considerably since they reached underground. They could not get to the lab quick enough. They continued down the straight path until Lucas stopped at a smaller side underpass. The underpass was below a four foot drop from the larger tunnel and continued straight on until it reached what looked like an air vent. Rebecca managed to squeeze aside Lucas inside the small underpass. She stared through the metal grill and saw the empty laboratory. The police had not yet found it. The trial patients were still in place, tied down to their blocks. Unconscious. Lucas carefully unlocked the grill and placed it to his side. The drop in front of them was almost sixty feet. There was nothing around to help them scale the drop.

"Well what now?" Rebecca asked.

Lucas reached into his suitcase and pulled out a thick rope with a claw attached to one end.

"You stay here, I'm gonna go down."

"Are we just going to leave everything the way it is?"

"Do you have any other suggestions?"

"I just thought we could do something about the patients. Try our best to hide it, for the other workers."

Lucas scratched his head and looked at the patients. "There isn't anything we can do without being caught." Lucas sighed. "I'm sorry Rebecca. We have to get the Grapheos and go."

Lucas turned his back to Rebecca and attached the claw to the end of the narrow underpass. Holding on to the rope he began to abseil into the lab. As he touched the bottom Rebecca drew a breath of relief. He ran over to his office and grabbed a locked silver box. He threw it up to Rebecca, who managed to catch it first time.

"Now listen carefully, I'm going to get on the end of the rope. I want you to pull as much as you can, okay?"

"Got it."

Rebecca pulled tight as Lucas placed his weight on the rope. But it was too much. The rope began to slip between the palms of her hands. Lucas could feel himself dropping.

"Rebecca pull!"

"I'm trying!" She replied, holding her breath.

"Attach the claw back."

Rebecca edged her way back and dragged the end of the rope on the end of the underpass. She held onto it tight as Lucas continued his journey back up and jumped onto the surface. They both stopped to catch their breath. Lucas could feel his heart beating through his chest. He looked down at the silver box they had just recovered.

"Is it inside?"

Rebecca unlocked the box and peered inside.

She nodded. "It's there. Are you sure you want to go? This is your last chance to back out."

Lucas continued to stare at the box. He shuffled his mouth and then looked at Rebecca. "We have to do this."

* * *

Malcolm waited for Lucas at the corner of 5th Street.

"Finally" He sighed as Lucas arrived before noticing someone else. "And you brought Rebecca."

"Nice to see you too Malcolm." Rebecca joked.

A black Mercedes saloon car pulled up beside them. Salazar rolled the slightly tinted driver's window down and peered at the group. He stopped and stared at Rebecca. It looked like he saw a ghost.

"Ella!? I... I thought you were dead?"

He had seen a ghost.

Biggest Regret

Adrian checked his Twitter feed for the tenth time in ten minutes. He folded his arms onto the desk and rested his head in between. It was another night where Adrian did not have any plans. His flatmates had invited him out but he was in no mood. Antony had been spending a lot of time trying to win over Alexa, much to Adrian's annoyance. He felt Antony was only thinking about himself which left him alone. He did not want to care, after all, Adrian was having fun with other friends. But he did care. This had to be the last night he was alone, Adrian needed his friend back. He picked up his mobile and stared at the bright screen. At the same time he heard a knock on his door. It was Jayden.

"Hey, are you not going out?" Jayden asked.

"No... why aren't you?"

"Had to stay late trying to get some work done with my group. Why aren't you out?"

"Just don't feel like it." Adrian sighed.

"Are you busy? Do you want to just hang out?"

"Yeah sure, come in."

Jayden entered Adrian's room and sat on his bed. Adrian sat down on his swivel chair and turned to Jayden.

"So why aren't you *really* going out?" Jayden leaned in closer.

Adrian shrugged. "It's stupid."

"It's Antony isn't it? I haven't seen him a lot either."

"You agree its ridiculous right?" Adrian lifted his shoulders and opened out his hands.

Jayden rolled his eyes. "To a certain extent."

"What does that mean?"

"Antony has every right to spend his time with whoever he wants. If he truly was one of your friends, then he'd be with you."

"Exactly, he's just being a dick."

"Have you actually explored the possibility he might be just that?"

"What do you mean?"

THE FRONT

"You haven't known anyone here for more than six months. Maybe that's the kind of person Antony is."

Adrian thought about Jayden's words for a moment. Then he uttered the words he never thought he would say.

"My best friend is a dick."

Adrian and Jayden started laughing. Jayden began to make another point.

"If you think about it, he's a bit of a loser. He has obviously, majorly entered the friend zone with this girl. I mean... they're not dating right?"

Adrian sniggered. "That's true. I think he's just really nervous to tell her the truth but he still loves to be around her."

"It's his loss." Adrian nodded. Jayden spread his arms out. "You still have us!"

Adrian smiled. "Thanks, I still think I should talk to him though. Maybe he doesn't realise what he's doing."

"Well good luck with that mate. So what do you wanna do?"

Adrian shrugged his shoulders. "Watch a film?"

"I know the perfect one." Jayden ran to his room and came back with a DVD held behind his back.

"It's not what I think it is, is it?"

Jayden pulled the DVD from behind his back and flashed it at Adrian "Saw II!"

"This probably won't help me sleep but fuck it!" Adrian grabbed the DVD and put the disc into his laptop. Jayden and Adrian spent the next couple of hours hooked to Adrian's laptop screen.

* * *

The following day Antony was alone in the kitchen preparing his lunch. He had also been texting Alexa. Adrian sat down at the table, his hands trembling.

"Hey." Antony acknowledged Adrian first.

"Hey... how was last night?" Adrian was hesitant to ask.

"It was fun. One of Alexa's friends passed out on an empty chair in the nightclub. One of the bouncers started shining a light in her eye!" Antony laughed.

Adrian chuckled along. "No way, was she okay?"

"Yeah she was singing along to the soundtrack in Maccies with us!"

"To be fair that is a good soundtrack!" Adrian exclaimed.

"What did you do?"

"To be honest I was bored. But Jayden came back from... I don't know... studying or whatever."

"Oh he has that group project doesn't he?"

"That's it. We watched Saw II!"

Antony's eyes lit up. "No way, which one is that again?"

"It's the one where the police guy's son is with that bunch of people. They're inhaling some kind of deadly gas."

"That movie always has such messed up storylines."

"Antony, it's all messed up. That's why we love it!" Adrian and Antony exchanged glances and laughed.

"You know, I wish I was watching it with you!"

Adrian stopped smiling and sighed. "Well... actually that's what I wanted to talk to you about."

Antony prepared his plate and walked over to the kitchen table. He placed his plate on the table and looked at Adrian with curious eyes.

"I think that... recently... you've been spending far too much time with Alexa." Adrian began.

Antony's facial expression became more serious.

"Take last night for example. We could have gone somewhere... a sports bar or something and just chilled out as buddies. Instead you went out with Alexa and all her girlfriends... and for what? To..."

Antony's speech became abrupt and angry. "To what Adrian? Go on, say what you have to say."

Adrian hesitated. "To be with a girl that... that... I don't think... is ever going to like you in the same way."

Adrian's words felt like a dagger to Antony's heart. "That's just what you would think isn't it? I have a real shot with a girl and you hate that."

"That's not what I'm saying at all!"

Adrian and Antony raised their voices.

"Yes it is. It's because you don't have a girl that you can spend time with. So you just want me to abandon ship by telling me you don't think I have a shot. Even if you did know a girl, you wouldn't have the confidence to be with her."

"I can't believe you just said that. That's coming from a guy that can't tell Alexa the truth and stop all this 'trying to win her over' bullshit."

"Am I the one that's bored every night? That's your issue."

"I was right. You are a dick."

"So now we move onto insults, pathetic!"

Adrian was astonished at Antony's reaction. "That's pathetic. I think that's what people would call someone that's been chasing a girl for months and is still in the friend zone."

Antony gritted his teeth at the notion. "How I choose to spend my time has nothing to do with you."

"You're really showing your true colours now aren't you!"

Antony let the silence fill the room for a few minutes. They exchanged angry stares before talking at a lower volume.

"Adrian listen, I really like this girl. And… it means a lot to be around her. That's why I choose to palm you off."

Adrian was stunned at what he was hearing. "Is that supposed to make me feel better? It just shows you have no consideration for anyone but yourself."

Antony lifted his arms and shrugged his shoulders. "Then I guess that's the way it is. Sorry."

It seemed there was no way to get through to Antony. Adrian only had one option left. "Then we can't be friends anymore."

Adrian stormed out the kitchen and slipped into his room, slamming the door behind him. Antony stayed isolated inside the kitchen to finish his meal. The silence only left Antony with broken thoughts. A friendship with many good memories, finished by a fractured one.

Adrian struggled to understand Antony's reaction. His best friend of the last six months had just completely changed. Best friends do not single out the weaknesses of their friends. That's what dominant people do. *Maybe Erik will be my only best friend?* To help Adrian deal with his thoughts, he decided to write in his diary.

BIGGEST REGRET

04/04/2015

Weakness — Weakness is showing too many negative emotions around other people. Showing weakness means you have lost faith. Positive faith. Not faith in an ideology that has negative consequences. You lose the faith that you will become the king, the queen, the explorer, the free thinker, the warrior, the game-changer or simply yourself. The life you want to live. If you are by yourself, then of course, you can let it all out. It is encouraged but for the needs of yourself and others, don't show weakness. Strength comes from within. It is not easy to get to. Some never find it.

- Adrian

Adrian liked to think he had more strength than most people. He had been through a lot and yet he still stood. He still wanted to better himself. But Adrian's biggest test of strength was still to come.

The Hardest Part

Antony lay on his bed, his feet rested on a pillow and his head faced the ceiling above. He was repeatedly throwing a small sponge ball against the wall and catching it. Antony struggled to see where Adrian's dark side had come from. Adrian was the kind of person that would only speak if it was important. He never actively looked for confrontation. *I did not do anything wrong. Adrian does not know me. What I've been through. He had no right to call me a dick.* He stopped bouncing the ball and stared at the picture of him and his family. *Maybe he did have a right? Maybe Adrian did have a point?* Antony had never stopped to consider Adrian had been through similar difficulties. It's what brought them together more than anyone else. It was easy to be caught up in your own world when you are fighting hard times. The more Antony thought about the situation, the more the guilt sank in. He had to go and apologise.

Antony picked himself up and walked towards Adrian's room. He knocked on his door three times. After a minute he heard Adrian come up and open the door. The two faced each other for a silent moment.

"Adrian, can I just talk to you." Antony pleaded.

Adrian sighed. "Aren't you supposed to be with Alexa?"

"Please?"

Adrian paused. "Sit down." He pulled to the side of the door to let Antony in.

Antony sat down on Adrian's bed and Adrian sat on his desk chair.

"I'm sorry I reacted the way I did. It was wrong to make them comments."

Adrian agreed with Antony. "I think we both said things we regret."

"When I think about it, I haven't been a good friend."

Adrian nodded. "I'm just relieved you finally see my side."

"Starting today, what do you wanna do?"

Adrian raised his head, smiling at Antony. "There's a game on…"

"Football, food and beer sounds good!"

"I can tell you've missed it! I'll give Jack a text."

Antony quietly laughed. Friendships are easy with the right people. It's finding the right people that is the hardest part.

* * *

Adrian, Antony and Jack decided to venture into the city of New York to find a different atmosphere to enjoy the game. After a wander they chose a sports bar called Woodwork. Woodwork offered a small and friendly atmosphere. The people seated at the bar could watch two large flat screen TV's at either side whilst it also presented another large screen and projector. The bar itself had a cosy feel mainly due to the wooden interior. The three students took their seats at a small table on the side, close to the third large TV screen.

"I'll get the first round!" Antony bellowed.

As the game wore on the table filled with a sharing plate of nachos, chips and 'cheezy' bread alongside the pile of empty pint glasses. Once the half-time break approached, Antony was fully soaking up the atmosphere.

"Guys this is so good!" Antony was sounding slightly intoxicated. Adrian and Jack exchanged grins with one another.

"How much fun are you having?" Adrian asked.

"So much fun. Just… to… come out with mates and chill out."

Jack and Adrian laughed.

"Seriously guys, I am so sorry for not doing this more."

Adrian looked back at Antony. "Well I'm glad you're finally realising it."

"Seriously, all that time I wasted with Alexa. It… jus' seems like a waste now."

"So much of a waste you had to say it twice." Jack joked.

Adrian offered his friend supporting words. "It wasn't a waste Antony. It's easy to get caught up in a first love."

"From now on I'm gonna offer my time to my best friends." Antony lifted his arms and wrapped them around Adrian and Jack who were sitting at his side.

"That's great big guy." Jack responded, lowering himself out of Antony's arm.

"I mean it. I won't be with stupid Alexa. Why the hell did I love her in the first place?"

THE FRONT

"You were just following instinct mate." Adrian replied.

"What even is love? Why do we feel things?" Antony continued to talk.

"Okay now it's getting too deep." Jack answered.

Adrian gave a better response. "That's the essence of love. No one understands it. It's just there."

"Why is it so important anyway?" Now Jack was asking stupid questions.

Adrian sighed and offered his best answer.

"Love makes us human. Everybody needs to be loved by someone and everyone needs to love someone. We all have our families. We use it to make new ones too."

"Dude that's beautiful." Antony reacted with a sarcastic and drunken tone.

"Now, I personally feel we should go back to watching the game before we start losing some serious man-points."

"Agreed." Jack nodded.

The students continued to gaze at the television, discussing the featured teams and players. Once the game had finished, the food had been eaten and the drinks were empty, they headed home, opting to walk back to the University together. Adrian kept his eye on Antony who began to resume the conversation they had earlier.

"Do you think I'm stupid?" He asked Adrian.

"What are you talking about? Why would I think that?"

"Well I convinced myself that I was in love with Alexa. What if I just made it up?"

Adrian shook his head. "I don't know how to respond to that. That's up to you to decide."

"What if everyone makes it up?" Antony challenged.

Adrian did not hold back his feelings. "The world is made up of liars. The truth is, most people don't meet the 'perfect' one. People just settle."

"I don't believe the 'perfect' one does exist." Jack muttered.

"I think you're right. We're humans. We do what we can to be happy and settle down."

"In the end we do fall in love with the person we're with." Antony offered some reassurance.

THE HARDEST PART

"We would do anything for them." Adrian added.

Antony smiled. "I think the moral of the story is to love, no matter what."

Adrian smirked. "You definitely got that from somewhere!"

"Fine. I heard it from a TED talk online."

"You watch TED talks too?" Adrian was surprised. "Guess you learn something new every day."

"They're interesting!" Antony yelled.

Adrian stepped away from Antony. "I didn't say they weren't!"

The three of arrived back at their flats and said their farewell to Jack. Antony and Adrian entered their empty and dark flat.

"It's dark." Antony stated.

"No shit Sherlock." Adrian replied as he reached the light switch. They both walked towards the kitchen to fill up glasses of water. Antony broke the silence.

"It's been a fun night. Thanks dude."

Adrian replied, apologetically. "I didn't mean to stop you from seeing Alexa at all. I just wanted the chance to do this sometimes."

Antony respectfully agreed. "Yeah I know. I was being a dick." Adrian stared at Antony before bursting into laughter.

"See you tomorrow mate."

Adrian left the kitchen and escaped into his room. Antony grabbed a seat at the table. He took a large sip of water from his glass and reflected on the earlier conversations.

Maybe it was all in his head?

Antony did not call it love until he thought it was love.

Love is not something you think you have. It's something that is just there. Without thinking about it.

The confrontation with Adrian was a wake-up call. It was time for him to start enjoying college properly, with his real friends. After all there were plenty more girls that Antony would be interested in. Antony had convinced himself that his love for Alexa was not real. His eyes had been opened.

I'm over her now.

THE FRONT

Antony's brain had taken over his heart. But when the heart knows what it wants, it will never rest. For Antony, that will be the hardest part.

Grapheos

"Ella... what are you talking about?" Lucas was confused with Salazar's reaction to seeing them. He looked at a dazed Rebecca hoping to make sense of the situation. Salazar had frozen, staring at the elegant, radiant statue of the woman in front of him. Ella was now in her early forties but in Salazar's eyes she did not look a day over twenty.

"Just get in the car!" Salazar shouted to the three scientists.

Malcolm opened the back door of the car and squeezed into the furthest seat. Rebecca and Lucas followed. The car silently drove away into the night.

"Is someone going to tell me what's going on?" Lucas asked.

"I have the same question Mr Arkwright." Salazar replied, training his eyes towards the front mirror. Rebecca was in the centre of his view.

"I'm back." Rebecca responded.

Lucas hoped for more information. "You're back?"

Rebecca sighed. "My name is not Rebecca, its Ella. I used to work for these guys a few years back."

"What even... how...?" Lucas' glare jumped between personnel in the car. "I don't know where to start." He was overloaded with more questions than answers.

"Why would you fake death, become a different person, only to return?" Salazar asked in a stern tone.

"We'll start with that." Lucas muttered.

Ella was exasperated by Salazar's question "You know I can't trust you!"

A mysterious voice interjected. "Then why are you back?" It came from the passenger seat in front of the trio.

"Who's this now?" Lucas asked.

"It's Simon, Salazar's sort of assistant." Ella whispered to a baffled Lucas.

"Simon, I... don't have any other options." Ella gently pushed her hair behind her ear.

Lucas continued to interrupt their reunion. "Hang on, why return as a scientist?"

Despite all the questions Rebecca remained calm. She had prepared for this. "When I decided to begin a new life, I wanted to do what I've always wanted. I'm fully qualified you know that. I started doing my dream job."

"How long ago were you with them?" Lucas pressed.

"Seven years ago. I was with them for four" Ella replied.

"What did you do with them? Was it a job?"

Ella exhaled. "I worked with them. I would help with their operations, you know…?"

"No unfortunately I'm not familiar with the workings of a gang." Lucas slouched back into his seat.

Malcolm perked up from his seat. "Would I be right in saying you faked your death to escape from these people?" He had finally caught up with the conversation.

"That's one way to look at it." Ella responded.

"Then what the hell are we doing here!?" Malcolm's threatening eyes glared at Lucas.

"I believe your friend has something special for us." Salazar further stoked the fires.

"You really going to give it to them?" Ella asked Lucas, visibly stressed.

"What are you talking about?" Malcolm asked.

Ella exhaled. "Lucas and I secretly developed a special device which could make our… goals achievable."

"And he's giving it straight to a gang. I didn't expect anything else!" Malcolm started to worry and continued to aim his emotion towards Lucas.

Lucas broke his silence as he tried to get back onto the side of his team. "I know this looks bad but trust me. Our dreams can be realised."

"How?" Malcolm continued to question Lucas' decisions.

"We know someone it could work on."

The car stopped. Salazar simply uttered the words, "We're here."

A young man dressed in a black suit opened the back door and gestured for the guests to leave the car. The trio found themselves in a garage alongside another black Mercedes car. Their eyes had to readjust to the sharpness and brightness of the light. They watched as a couple of beefy mechanics ran towards the car before they were quickly ushered through another door. They had entered a dark hallway filled with flickering lights coming from different rooms.

"In here." The young man pointed directly to the door on their left. They were faced with three fierce looking gang members, wearing black vests and ripped jeans. They were deep in conversation before pausing and glaring at the scientists who dared go any further than the doorway. Each gang member had tattoos running down their arms and faces full of scars. One of the tattoos included the gang's portrayal of the Mexican ghost. This was the visual of a skeleton wearing a large sombrero below three patterned bells. The skeleton was wearing an open ripped suit that showed its bare boned rib cage. The Mexican ghost was a common image worn by members of the gang who originated from Mexico. It was their secret way of belonging to a sub group within the gang. It terrified their latest guests, even Ella. It had been a couple of years since she faced the characters that dominated her previous life. Even at her highest level in the group she was still uneasy around the tough and sinister exterior of the other members. They were people that only knew violence and crime. They had never been taught emotions and empathy. They were simply not human.

"Dejarlos solos!" The young man shouted at the gang members who proceeded to make their way towards the trio and out the door. The young man then left and closed the door behind them. The three scientists looked at each other before moving further into the empty room.

"What did he say?" Lucas asked.

"It's Spanish. He told them to leave us alone." Ella replied.

The room they were left in was barely furnished. There was only two things in sight; a falsely positioned sofa being used as something to lean on rather than sit on and a large table in the centre of the room holding paperwork, cigarette butts and cash. The window at the far end had been boarded up. The only light in the room was a dim yellow haze provided by a bulb hanging from the ceiling. Ella and Malcolm leaned against the sofa and Lucas sat above the table. They were all still trying to make sense of the situation.

"Well, I don't think we will be found here." Malcolm stated.

Ella scouted the room. "I don't miss places like this."

"Would you live here? You know… eat and sleep." Lucas asked.

"A lot of the gang members have other lives. Some have families. They have nice homes to go to, including me."

"Why did you stop trusting them?"

"I never did trust them. My husband disappeared about five years ago. I think they were involved."

Malcolm quickly stopped Ella. "Wait, why did you wait a couple of years before you escaped?"

Ella was exasperated with all the questions. "I had to wait for the perfect opportunity! I couldn't just disappear straight after my husband. It was too risky."

"Well, now they know the truth. What's stopping them from punishing you?"

Ella turned her back to Malcolm and Lucas. She gazed upon the boarded window with a distressed look. "Nothing." Her hands began to shake. "That's why I'm worried."

Lucas and Malcolm exchanged concerning looks. They had no idea what they had gotten themselves into.

* * *

Simon followed Salazar back to his makeshift office. The broken door hung against its hinges as the light found its way into the dark lair. A half empty suitcase lay open at the side of the room. In the centre of the room on top of a grand wooden table was a map of the North East of the US with red circles drawn over distinct towns and cities. Simon and Salazar both rested side by side against the table. They had a lot to discuss.

"What do you think?" Salazar had to be the first to speak out of respect.

"I think she blames us. It's clear now." Lucas whispered.

"Do you think I made a mistake?"

"Doing what?"

"Bringing them here?"

"You could see it that way. But maybe this is an opportunity." Simon's eyes widened. "We can all get closure from this. Instead of running away. This is our chance of confronting the problem."

"What do you think of Lucas and the other one?"

"It sounded like they have something to show you. Something big. If it's successful we could finally restart a viable business." Simon stopped for a moment. He muttered under his breath. "With someone that could protect our assets."

Salazar remained deep in thought. Simon's advice and opinions were just as important to him as his own. He had to collect his thoughts and make some decisions.

"We should go and talk some more with the group." Salazar whispered. Simon agreed and the two of them walked across the hallway to their room.

The group paused their conversation and looked at Salazar and Simon as they entered the room. Salazar gazed at Ella, before talking to Lucas instead.

"Lucas, how has business been?"

"Not good. We haven't been able to create a formula that works. One patient escaped yesterday and burned alive in the street. It's blown the lid all over the project."

"Burned alive?"

"Yes, when the patients are with us we also give them a counter agent so they can be eased into the formula. When they stop having that the pure energy takes over and it becomes too much. They are burned from the inside. All the casualties have resulted in this way."

"Interesting. So, what is this special device you have to show me?"

Lucas jumped off the table and grabbed his suitcase on the side. He opened it up and pulled out a silver box. He released the two locks and looked up at Salazar.

"This."

Salazar stared at the thin band in front of him. It glowed a deep red colour that almost looked alive. The band was made to fit on the wrist and had small sharp ends. Lucas' face beamed with excitement. He savoured the moment he could finally share this with someone else. "It's called Grapheos. It combines the pure energy formula we have been researching with the so-called miracle material, Graphene."

"What does it do?"

Lucas' smile faded. He felt insulted until he remembered where he was. "The ends connect to the bloodstream and delivers small doses of the energy. The Graphene enables it to be smart. It can connect to the internet and provide real-time information."

Salazar picked up the band and inspected it closely. "Like your experiment, this is essentially a ticking bomb for whoever wears it?"

Lucas tilted his head. "Well we haven't tested it yet. It could work or it could kill."

Salazar cracked a smile. "I like the odds."

"That is a really advanced piece of kit you know? Don't waste it." Ella exclaimed.

Salazar placed the device back in the box and approached Ella.

"I think it's time for a chat." Salazar attempted to intimidate Ella.

But it seemed in vein. "You don't scare me."

"Would you mind telling me why you felt the need to fake your own death to get away from us then?"

Ella inched away. "I know you did it. At the very least you were involved in Peter's disappearance."

Salazar opened out his arms. "We have told you many times, we did not do anything! Peter was just as valuable to us as he was to you."

"Why don't I believe you?"

Salazar glanced around the room. "Look at this Ella. We were great before. Since Peter disappeared we are runners. We live in… this…"

Ella was not convinced. "This is what you do. You manipulate people to get your way. You think I'm just going to blindly follow your words?"

"I don't want you to follow us Ella. I want to you to follow the truth."

"You know what? I… I don't care if I put my own life at risk. It's time you were put away for good!"

Ella began to storm out of the room but she was met with two of the large gang members from before.

Salazar crossed his hands across his large build. "We cannot allow that. I'm sorry but we can't trust your freedom."

The two men grabbed each of Ella's arms. Ella struggled to break free.

"What are you doing?" Lucas cried as he moved towards Ella.

"Relax Mr Arkwright, we are just taking her to her bedroom."

"Get off me!" Ella's shouting was simply background noise.

"If you don't return her immediately you are not getting hold of anything of mine!"

Salazar stopped Ella and the men. He stared at Lucas and raised his eyebrows. "Mr Arkwright, this will be beneficial to you too."

Lucas was confused. "What do you mean?"

"I believe we are both chasing the same boy, correct?"

"Boy!?"

"The one that was getting in my way. The one that knows about your project. The special one that could finally fulfil your dreams. Ella's son of course."

Lucas stood still. Frozen.

"No, not Adrian! Lucas please!" Ella pleaded.

Lucas looked to the ground. His mind was searching for an answer. The Grapheos had great potential. Everything he had worked for could finally be vindicated.

"If it works, your project will be successful." Salazar was pressuring Lucas' decision.

"Why can Ella not stay with us?" He asked.

Salazar answered. "Look at her. This is family. She will do whatever she can to protect him. If you are going to take this risk then she needs to be under control."

Lucas took another minute before uttering the words Ella feared.

"Let's bring him in."

Au Revoir

Antony could not believe what he was seeing. He was sure it was her. *Alexa.* The day reached midnight. He was about to get into bed. As he closed the curtains he glanced out of the window. What he saw was a couple holding hands and walking away to the opposite block. Low lights lit up the pathway outside revealing the full complexion of Alexa. But he could not see the man. It did not matter. Antony still felt the pain in his heart. Over the past week he was convinced he was over her. But his reaction said otherwise. He still had feelings for her. *How stupid could I be?* His head was overloaded with thoughts spiralling through every conceivable series of events throughout the night. The time could not have passed slower. He watched his alarm clock pass through the hours. The sun was beginning to rise and shine through his curtains. He could hear movement inside the flat. Someone had come through the flat door and sneaked straight into their room. Antony checked the time again. *6:06*. It was too early to get up. The restlessness was getting to him. He had to try and get some sleep.

Antony's pulse slowed. His body began to rest. His breathing was minimal. Then his eyes shot open. His body lifted upwards and his breathing increased uncontrollably. A nightmare. *It was just a nightmare.* He glared at his alarm clock again. *10:04*. He brought his legs forward and sat up on his bed, taking a sip of water from a glass beside his bed. He decided to go to the kitchen to see if anyone was there.

"Hey." The voice that greeted him was Adrian's.

Adrian had already showered and was cooking a fry-up. He stood by the cooker wearing grey converse shoes and slightly faded grey jeans. On top he wore a plain white t-shirt covered by a deep blue hoodie.

Antony rubbed his eyes to wake himself up more.

"Hey." Antony replied. He walked straight over to his cupboard and grabbed a cereal box and a bowl.

"Are you all right?" Adrian sensed something was not quite right.

Antony poured some milk into his bowl, placed it on the table and pulled out a chair. He dipped his spoon into the bowl and slowly crunched the cereal inside his mouth.

"I saw… Alexa with another guy last night."

Adrian quickly turned around. "Another guy? Did you see who it was?" He stepped towards Antony.

"No I couldn't see him. But I know it was her."

Adrian carefully backed away. "Big deal I thought you were over her now?"

Antony dropped his spoon and glared at Adrian. "Well I'm not. It's not going away."

Adrian sighed. The two of them were distracted by the kitchen door as Jayden walked in, dressed casually in blue chinos and a navy blue polo shirt.

"What are you girls moaning about now?" Jayden joked.

Adrian widened his eyes at Jayden. "Antony saw Alexa with another guy." Adrian answered

"Oh man, drop it."

"Jayden I've tried." Antony replied.

"This is a good thing. You should be happy for her. This is a real chance for you to move on."

"I want to but it should be me!" Antony buried his head into his hands.

"Just face it. You didn't do enough. Get over it." Jayden took a seat next to Antony.

Antony nodded. "You're right. I didn't do enough. I don't deserve her."

"You see this. The only reason you're so hurt by this is because you regret not doing enough to be that guy. It could have been you. It might not have been. I guess you'll never find out."

"Are you saying I should tell her? Get some closure?"

Jayden spoke with a measure of confidence. "Before it gets serious with this guy, I think it's a good idea. But not right now. Give yourself some time."

"How long?"

"I think we all need some cheering up. Guess what just opened at East 86th Street Cinema?" Jayden asked.

Adrian looked excited. "Oh god you haven't?"

THE FRONT

"What?" Antony was curious.

"I got us tickets to the Avengers 2 showing later!"

Jayden held out his palm as Adrian gave him a high five.

"Okay that's pretty awesome." Admitted Antony.

* * *

The three flatmates arrived at East 86th Street Cinema after a beautiful long walk across Manhattan Park. The evening drew nearer as the sunset glistened through the trees and the green turned orange. Antony's spirits had been lifted whilst Adrian and Jayden were excited for the movie. East 86th was a large establishment. On the outside, it had the 'Broadway' styled movie listings. The main entrance lay deep into the building where movie posters surrounded them. Upon entrance Jayden approached reception to collect their tickets. Adrian and Antony stayed back and gazed upon the cinema. They had never been to a theatre like this before and they were amazed at the size of it. There were a lot of places in America that caught Adrian's imagination. They were usually large and full of history. Some of them were an amazing feat of achievement by human kind.

Above the paying counters was a large arc that encompassed the main part of cinema. The inside of the arc was plain white which allowed lights at reception to shine upon it and create a starry effect. The main section consisted of the main counter, a fun zone which had air hockey tables and arcade games and a confectionary shop. The screens were split into two zones, zone one was on the left and zone two on the right. Altogether the cinema could boast fifteen cinema screens. Once Jayden returned with the tickets the trio made their way to screen six. When they entered they found themselves at the back of room with the screen at the bottom of several steps. The steps were lit on the sides not dissimilar to an airport runaway. The colours interchanged between orange and red with each passing row. The cinema screen covered most of the back wall which was comparable in size to around thirty columns of seats.

The students took seats three rows from the back. Soon the screening room filled up and the anticipation grew around the whole room. With a quick glance around them they could see children in 'Iron Man' masks and several 'Thor' hammers hitting the air. The start of the film was greeted with an applause.

* * *

"I have visual."

Simon stood at the corner of East 86th Street in New York. He quietly uttered his words into the hand-held transmitter he was holding. Wrapped around his shoulder was a plain black flight bag containing his equipment. As Adrian, Jayden and Antony crossed the road to start their journey home, Simon followed at a safe distance.

"Signal when they enter." Salazar replied. He and his team waited around the corner from the great Manhattan Park. In the passenger seat was Lucas and behind him were two of his gang goons.

"They're approaching the park entrance now." That was the signal for Salazar and his men to prepare.

They abandoned the car and headed through the park. The darkness disguised them and the lack of security camera's made it the perfect spot for a kidnapping. Lucas was carrying a 'Diversion' sign under his arm until they reached their stopping point. He dropped the sign in the middle of the small path and pointed it to a smaller path leading to a large circle of concrete and a dead end. As the team scampered between the trees with a full view of the centre circle, they each pulled on a mask. Commonly known as 'Guy Fawkes Masks' in modern times they are associated with the internet hacking group 'Anonymous'. Deceiving and haunting, the mask was a clean white with black eyebrows, a magicians' moustache and a goatee. Once they found a comfortable position the two gang members and Lucas pulled out a rifle and rested it on sniper rifle holders.

Adrian, Jayden and Antony walked along the path until they reached the sign. At first they were curious.

"This wasn't here before." Adrian stated.

"Maybe something happened. Let's just follow the diversion." Antony countered.

They turned left and continued on through the smaller path. After a couple of minutes they stood in the centre circle and looked at each other.

"It's a dead end!" Adrian retorted.

Antony stared at Adrian. He started shaking and pointed to his neck.

"What is it?" Adrian asked.

"Your neck." Antony was panicking.

Adrian looked to his side and saw a long silver plated dart with a red coated end. It had pierced through his skin painlessly. Adrian suddenly felt weak. His vision became blurred until it eventually disappeared into darkness. Jayden and Antony could only watch as he hit the ground unconscious. They were soon interrupted by the voices of others.

"Dammit how did you both miss?" Lucas shouted at the two thugs. Antony and Jayden recoiled in horror as they saw the masks and the sniper rifles.

"What have you done!?" Antony shouted.

"Relax kid you'll forget all about it."

Lucas lifted his rifle up and pointed it at Antony. At the same time another thug pointed his gun towards Jayden. Without hesitation they pulled the trigger and sent them falling to the floor. The students were placed in separate bags and carried to the car. Mission accomplished.

Ordinary Human

Adrian sensed the feeling of Déjà vu overcome his mind and soul. He had woken up hung against the wall of an unknown room. His wrists, ankles and neck were all clamped against the wall with large metal straps. The room was around ten foot tall. Adrian could see a small window at the top to the wall adjacent to him. It was still dark. The room was lit by a tube light in the centre of the ceiling and provided a deep red glow. Directly ahead of him was a thick heavily locked door. Adrian searched through his mind for answers. He could not remember how he got here. The last memory he could recall was being in the cinema with Antony and Jayden. *Antony and Jayden.* Adrian wondered if they had been involved. *Are they okay? Are they here?* Someone was clearly after him and he had no idea why. He started hearing noises from the large door. Small subtle movements coupled with sounds that were getting louder. His anticipation grew. Someone was coming in.

One final click and the large door peered open. White light started to escape through one degree at a time. Adrian began to turn his head away from the bright light until his eyes adjusted properly. Then he saw a large shadow carefully block out the light. A large man emerged, dressed smartly with a stern expression on his face. Two other men followed, one was bulkier and intimidating. The other was smaller and looked more intelligent. He was carrying a small silver case.

Salazar greeted Adrian first. "Adrian, it's so nice to finally meet you."

"Who are you?" Adrian asked. Despite his question, Adrian recognised Lucas and Salazar.

"Let's not pretend."

Adrian tried to break his wrist free from the straps but struggled. "Seriously I don't know who you are!"

Salazar sighed. "My name is Roberto Salazar and my gang is known as Sinaloa Cartel."

"As you already know my name is Adrian and I was minding my own fucking business when I woke up here!"

Adrian's arrogant tone made Salazar chuckle. "Can we please let the boy down?"

Another bulky man stomped into the room and helped the other unscrew Adrian from the metal shackles. Once free, Adrian took a swipe at one of the thugs. He fell to the floor holding his face, blood visibly pouring out of his nose. Lucas, Salazar and the other gang member immediately produced a gun and aimed it at Adrian's face. Adrian stopped and glanced around.

Salazar had stopped smiling. "I give you freedom. Respect it."

Adrian lowered his fists. "What do you want?"

"You're a special person Adrian."

Adrian rolled his eyes at Salazar. "How so?"

"My friend here, Lucas, has something special he would like to test on you."

"I'm not a lab rat!" Adrian blurted.

"But the effects Adrian. They will be very beneficial to you." Salazar continued.

"I'm sorry mister but I'm quite content with my life at the moment."

Salazar smirked. "You don't get it." He placed the palm of his hand onto Adrian's face. "You don't have an option."

Adrian's smile faded. "Just answer me one thing."

"What?"

"My friends, Antony and Jayden. Are they okay?"

"We left them in a safe place. They won't remember anything." Salazar kept the gun pointing barely an inch from Adrian's face. "Now, Lucas is going to run some tests on you. Don't try anything please. Or a bullet will piece your skull. We won't hesitate." Salazar loomed over Adrian. He stared at the teenager with a sinister smile before strutting out the room.

The past was finally catching up with Adrian.

* * *

Ella had been locked in the same room for twenty-four hours. She was trapped in a moderately sized chamber, placed in between a double bed in the centre and a small TV alongside a monitor. The lifeless walls were hardly covered by the falling wallpaper and crumbling brown plastering. Ella had only managed a few hours' sleep. She spent her time wondering why she chose to return. *It was a stupid decision.* Whatever decision she made, they would have gone after Adrian. At least this way she would be close to him and had a chance of keeping him safe. Ella was watching Adrian on a small monitor despite him being kept just thirty feet below her. At this stage reasons for optimism were slowly deteriorating but seeing Adrian demonstrate some fight gave her hope. Lucas was focused on the monitoring devices attached to electrodes on Adrian's head. The heavy door behind her scraped open. She watched the guard let Salazar through.

"What do you want?" Ella turned her back to Salazar and continued to watch the monitor.

"I just wanted to see how you were doing. Are you enjoying the show?" Salazar moved closer. "You can stop this."

Ella looked back at him, curious. "How?"

"That band will certainly kill him."

"Then why did you *really* bring Adrian here?"

Salazar's ruthless voice turned soft. "Ella, I want you and Adrian to join us."

Ella shrugged off the suggestion. "Why would I do that?"

"We can offer you a good life," he stressed. "With Adrian we can live the life we could only dream of before."

"You have to be kidding." Ella laughed, sarcastically. "How can you think I would choose to stay with you let alone my son too?"

"Adrian has abilities Ella you know that. He could help us reach the top."

"The answer is no." Ella was stern. "You have to let us go and live normal lives. You took away my husband. I'm not letting you take away us too!"

"How many times do we have to tell you? We had no involvement in that!" Salazar insisted.

"And you expect me to believe you!"

Salazar sat down beside Ella and grabbed her hand.

"Get off me." Ella shouted pulling her hand away.

"Ella, there is another reason I want you to stay."

"What now?" Ella muttered.

"We can be... be together."

Ella inched away from Salazar. Her mind was struggling to make sense of him. "What do you mean? What are you saying?"

Salazar took a deep breath. "Ella," he whispered. "I love you."

Ella was stunned. "You... you creep." She held her hand over her mouth and pushed herself further from Salazar. "Oh my god... is that why you got rid of Peter?"

Salazar instantly shook his head. "What? No of course not. I don't know what happened to Peter!"

"No, this isn't happening. I don't care about your feelings or whatever. I just want to get away from here. Let me go!" Ella stormed towards the door to escape. Salazar rose from the bed with intent based on outrage. He confronted Ella with a dark temper and alarming voice.

"You are not going anywhere! I've had enough." He grasped her arm and shifted her away from the door. "You will be part of my gang. You and your son."

Ella gritted her teeth. "And what if I say no?"

Salazar paused and lowered his tone. "Then I will personally kill Adrian with your own invention. You can watch him cry in pain." Salazar crept closer to Ella's face as he towered above her. "There will be nothing you can do about it."

Ella backed away from the door. She did not want to let her fear control her life anymore. She believed in Adrian. Enough to make one of the toughest decisions she ever made. "Go ahead."

Salazar was caught by surprise. "What?"

Ella shrugged. "Give Adrian the Grapheos. No more waiting." She peered into Salazar's cold eyes. "Kill him."

"You really think he will survive?" Salazar grinned. "Pathetic. Your own son's death will be on your conscious." He brushed past Ella and left the room.

Ella calmly sat back down and watched the monitor. Hoping. Praying that she made the right decision.

Salazar burst through the chamber door and charged down the stairs. He took a U-turn at the bottom and headed through the door to the cellar. As he descended down the stairs he could see Lucas still attaching wires to

Adrian and watching his monitors. Salazar stormed straight towards the small silver box. Lucas hastily stood up and gazed at him.

"What are you doing?" Lucas could see the rage that had built up inside him.

"Forget the tests we're using this now." He tore open the box and ripped out the Grapheos.

"But... the risks?"

"We don't care about that now. That kid needs to finally prove himself." Salazar was on edge. Lucas could not stop him.

Adrian stood up and kicked away his chair. As an adrenaline-fueled Salazar approached him he took a weak swing at his head. But the blood loss weakened him. Salazar took hold of Adrian's swinging hand and pinned it against the wall. He lifted his left arm and forced the Grapheos band against Adrian's wrist. The band reacted and the two pins pierced Adrian's veins wide-open before closing tight. He could only scream as Salazar backed away and watched him suffer.

Adrian's pupils disappeared into his brain. His body started to violently shake until he dropped to the floor. Salazar, Lucas and the others all gazed at Adrian as he lay still. Ella watched on in horror. She held her hands together and willed Adrian to stand up. But he did not. After a long and gruelling minute Salazar turned to the camera.

"Happy now?"

Tears started to roll down Ella's face. She was more than upset. She was angry. She wanted to be by her son's side in his last minutes. She stood up and ran over to the door. A guard burst in and grabbed her arms. He pushed her onto a metal chair and strapped in her wrists and ankles as she screamed out the door.

"You fucking bastard! You will pay for this you son-of-a-bitch!"

Downstairs, everyone continued to stare at Adrian. This could not be the end. The silence only made more noise. Then Ella's prayers were answered. The band on Adrian's left wrist began to beat, on and off. The deep red glow shined and then faded repeatedly. It was mimicking his heartbeat. Lucas stepped back. Ella clenched her fists. Salazar was anxious. Adrian was still alive.

Run

The band sustained its rhythm. A fearful Salazar signalled his gang to raise their guns but hold fire. "He's not moving. Why isn't he moving?"

Lucas froze. He was reminded of the horrific death of Patient 31.

Adrian's eyes suddenly shot open. He soured to his feet and glanced at the crowd ahead of him.

Salazar still held fire.

Adrian fixed his eyes on him. His stare isolated Salazar in a state of pure terror. Adrian grasped his neck, gripping tightly to lift him up. With his last breath Salazar gestured for his gang to open fire. But it was useless. The bullets could not penetrate Adrian's miracle skin. Adrian grasped Salazar's neck tighter. And tighter. Then like a rag doll Adrian tossed him aside. Salazar crashed into a wall that collapsed around him. The large man fainted as he fell to the floor.

Adrian shifted his attention to the heavy door in front of him. Cowering in fear, the remaining members of the gang parted ways and allowed Adrian to drift through them and climb the stairs. He pushed open the front door to the hideout sending it soaring off into the night air. Adrian stepped outside and lowered his knees. The power of the Grapheos had taken complete control of him. His fist stuck to the ground and his head lifted up to the dark sky. A surge of wind started to envelop the air around him. Nobody could get near him. The ground beneath him shook vigorously and within seconds Adrian shot into the air and disappeared.

Lucas, Simon and the other gang members could only stare in complete silence, in a state of disbelief. After a moment Simon finally brought himself back down to Earth and his focus switched to his boss, Salazar. He ran back inside, gently approaching the static and broken figure. Simon placed two fingers beneath his head to check his pulse. There was a slow but sharp beat.

"We need to get him all the medic supplies we can find. Someone help me lift him!" Simon shouted at the top of his lungs.

The others helped Simon lift Salazar up and placed him on a table another gang thug had wheeled in.

"Lucas you're a scientist, please help." Simon pleaded.

Lucas was still in a state of shock but he agreed to help save his fallen friend. A frantic Simon then rushed up the stairs to ask for more help from an unlikely source.

"Ella, you have to help!" Simon exclaimed as he erupted through the door.

Ella smirked at the desperate man. "You think I'm going to help. My son gave him exactly what he deserved."

"Ella, Salazar gave you a lot, he needs you!"

"Tell him something for me." She moved closer to Simon. "Never underestimate my son again."

The irritated assistant looked to the guard by her side. "Keep her tied up. We'll deal with her later."

Ella screamed like she had gone insane. "Do whatever you want with me! My son is far away from you, that's all that matters!"

* * *

Union Street was one of the parts of Jersey City that was broken. Cracked roads and troubled company, Jersey City sat in the shadow of the big apple across the river from Manhattan. Today, it stood quiet and uneventful. But Adrian soon changed that. A loud crash echoed across the block as he collided with the ground, rebounding a few more yards before stopping. Adrian groaned in pain as he peered over to the further damage he had caused to the road. He curled up holding his arm in distress. His mouth was clenched and his eyes were closed tightly. Breathing heavily, he rolled onto his back and tilted his head onto the road. But the time to rest had to wait. In the surrounding houses he could see lights illuminate the street. The local residents were waking up. Adrian shuffled onto his feet as quick as he could. With pain still burning through his legs he hobbled to a nearby alleyway to hide. It gave him a chance to gather his thoughts.

Whatever this band was, it had given him enormous power. As soon as it touched him he changed into someone else. *Something else.* Only now was he feeling like himself again. Then the memories came flooding back. The house, the horror in everyone's eyes. Staring at a man fearing for his life and then tossing him aside like his existence never mattered. As he collapsed to the side of a dumpster, Adrian wondered if the man had survived. But that did not matter anymore. He was stuck in the middle of nowhere, alone. Adrian studied the band on his wrist. It was beating at an increasing rate. At the top he could see a word carved into the material. *Grapheos.* Another name was etched to the side. *Trinity.* Adrian had no idea what these words meant. He questioned what else the band could do. As he touched the front panel a message flew by the screen.

Welcome

Small 'App' style icons layout vertically down his wrist. Adrian was drawn to the icon at the bottom, a simple outline of a heart. This app brought up information about his vital signs, blood levels and dose level. Another icon showed him map information and used GPS to mark his location to within a few feet. Adrian began to realise the band was a real piece of advanced kit. But the motions Adrian was making. That was him. *Did I seriously just fly? Could I do it again?* The question lingered on his mind. He crouched onto the ground and placed both his fists on the cobbled stones. He closed his eyes and could sense his heart beating faster. Adrian could feel the power overwhelm his internal system. He shot his head up expecting to be surrounded by clouds. He dreamed of being closer to the moon. But when he opened his eyes, he had not moved. It was the same alleyway. The same dumpster. He tried again. Nothing. *I cannot fly.*

Adrian was frustrated, isolated and far away from home. It seemed the night was finally taking its toll as he kicked out at the nearby dumpster. The dumpster flew through the air and landed around ten metres from where he was standing. It seemed what Adrian did have was enormous strength and energy. It was not the best way to test his skill though. Soon, the local residents crowded around the beaten waste container and noticed Adrian alone in the alleyway. They quickly circled the lonely teenager. Adrian paused as the small gathering of strangers stared at him. A small voice echoed from the back.

"Why did you throw our dumpster?"

Adrian did not know how to respond. The line of people he faced waited for an answer.

"I…" He glanced around the alleyway. It was a dead end. "I don't know."

Another moment of silence followed. Adrian backed away a couple of inches. As he watched the crowd, he noticed a women's face focused on his band. The beating light stayed constant. But it gave Adrian an idea. He promptly turned his back to the crowd and ran towards a high staircase hanging from the building. He jumped onto the end and used his power to pull himself and climb towards the roof. The crowd watched him reach the top in silence. No action was taken. No word was spoken.

Adrian pulled himself over a small wall and landed feet first onto the roof of the building. A full moon gleamed in the night sky. The view was spectacular. Towering above the small-scale Jersey City was the infamous bright lights of New York City. The palms of Adrian's hands rested on the back of his head. He had to take a moment to admire the elegance that embraced his eye line. The haze of light engulfed the city like a halo, protecting the diverse and delicate architecture. The white light shimmering down from the moon interlaced with the city lights to produce a smooth, dark and luxurious colour. This was a special view. On a personal level, it made Adrian think about the bigger world he was a part of. There were millions of people ahead of him but only he had the band. A band so powerful it could change the world.

Adrian peered over the small wall that surrounded him. The drop was deep. He stepped over to the other side of the roof and focused on the building forty feet away from where he was. He puffed out his chest and began running at full speed. As he reached the wall he leaped into the air. He pushed one leg onto the wall, using it as leverage to increase the power in his leap. Adrian hung more than hundred feet in the air, accelerating towards a second roof. A smile arose on his face as he landed. The power felt incredible. It was invigorating. Adrian fist-pumped the air and faintly laughed under his breath. But he still had no idea where he was. He looked around at the other buildings until he remembered what his band could do. Bringing up the GPS, Adrian set a course for his college home.

Adrian began sprinting towards the end of the wall again. But there was a problem. The band began to blink far too quickly. Soon it completely switched off. There was no display and no glow. Adrian was stuck in mid-air about to come crashing down to Earth. As he fell towards his target, Adrian managed to grab hold of a gutter on top of a house. Using his strength he rotated himself into a nearby window. He smashed through the glass and landed on his side. Adrian could feel the pain of his tearing skin soar through his body. He could feel glass pieces stuck in his back as he lay on top of them. He gently opened his eyes to a small boy sat up in his bed peering at him. He lifted himself up and looked at the boy. The child looked about ten years old and was clutching a small teddy bear in his left hand.

"Hey kid."

The boy threw his teddy at Adrian.

"Who the fuck are you?"

Adrian took another look at the boy. He was not expecting that response.

"Sorry, I'll get out of your way," Adrian replied as he walked slowly across the room still in significant pain.

He gently climbed out the window and decided to jump the short distance to the ground once the band turned back on. He could hear the boy's parents scream as they entered his room. It was still a couple of hours before dawn and the streets were deserted. Adrian needed to assess the device. As he stepped through the barren street he felt his wrist jolt. Then his body. In shock, Adrian hit the floor. He held his wrist in agony. He could not control his movements. The pain spread through his body like wildfire. The band was unstable. Adrian knew had to learn more about exactly what he had been forced to wear or he faced certain death.

Changes

"Kiss me Antony." Alexa's beautiful face sparkled in the sunset light. The ocean glistened. The trees moved gently. The scene was picture perfect. Antony brought his lips closer to hers. He closed his eyes as they moved closer. But they never touched. Centimetres away, Antony started feeling a sharp pain in his chest. Alexa backed away. Antony gazed upon her as she disappeared into the air. The pain became more severe. Antony opened his mouth but he could not speak. He held his chest and groaned. The pain gradually worked its way upwards until it reached his head.

Antony opened his eyes. He faced a coin that a passing pedestrian had just thrown at him. As he lifted his head he stared closely at the person walking away. It was still dark so all he could see was the small street light reflection off a handbag they were holding. He turned his attention to his surroundings. He was leaning against a building and a street that he was familiar with. But he did not know why he recognised it. *Where am I?* Antony then took another look around. He saw the entrance to a building and instantly realised where he was. *That's it, I live here.* He walked over the entrance, picked out his lanyard key from his pocket and entered the building block. Once he reached his flat he could see the kitchen light shining through the window to the corridor. Antony found Jayden in the kitchen who greeted him with a wide smile.

"Am I relieved to see you?"

Antony held his head as he felt it pounding. "What the hell happened?"

Jayden shrugged. "I have no idea. The last thing I remember is the cinema."

"Maybe we had a spontaneous night out?" Antony suggested.

"It's the only reason I can find for waking up on the street." Jayden sighed. He was disappointed with himself.

"You woke up on the street too?"

"Yeah. We must've had a lot." Jayden paused. "I mean a lot."

Antony nodded. "Have you seen Adrian?"

"I think he is in his room sleeping. Best wait till tomorrow if we wake him."

Antony agreed. "Well... I'm gonna go to bed properly now. In my own bed."

Jayden laughed. "See you in the morning."

Antony traipsed into his room. His head was feeling heavy and his eyes had to work hard to stay open. It took him a long few seconds to put his key in the right place before eventually managing to open his door. He fell straight onto his bed and lay down under the covers. He felt the stress lift from his head as it hit the soft, cosy pillow. His dreary eyes gently closed as he was whisked away back into a dream.

Antony was lying on a quiet beach. It was sunrise. The stunning tint of orange twinkled off the ocean. The light was reflecting off the glass of juice he and Alexa were sharing. They stared back at each other. They both leaned in for the kiss. Antony closed his eyes. But nothing. Alexa was backing away. She picked up the glass and poured the juice out on the sand in-between them. She peered at Antony with harrowing eyes. Then she squeezed the palm of her hand. As the pressure increased, the glass smashed. Antony could see shards of glass penetrate her skin and bleed out of her fingers.

"What the fuck!?" Antony instantly awoke to his bedroom window smashing. Glass was scattered across his floor and in the midst a man lay still.

"Wait..." Antony recognised him. "Adrian?"

Adrian groaned in pain. "Hey man. Sorry about this." He gazed around at the mess he had made in his friend's bedroom.

Antony was completely and utterly baffled "I don't even know where to start!"

Adrian stood up and stared at Antony. "We can start with you getting your lazy ass out of bed!" He gently picked some glass out of his clothes.

"Oh of course. It's not like there is FUCKING GLASS ALL OVER MY FLOOR!"

Adrian smiled. "Okay, I said I'm sorry."

Antony shook his head. "Why are you appearing through my window? You look like you've just been to the moon and back."

"It's a long story. Can I use your computer? And use you on your computer…?"

Antony still had a lot of questions. He navigated past the glass and sat down at his computer. "I think it's a story worth telling."

"Well I don't remember being knocked out or whatever but I woke up in some house tied up."

"You were tied up!?"

"They let me loose afterwards. There were these huge guys guarding the doors and then this scientist starts doing tests on me. He attached wires all over me."

"This sounds like a bad dream." Antony butted in.

"Will you let me finish?" Adrian gave Antony a stern look.

"I'm sorry carry on."

"Okay so this guy is doing tests on me. Then this fat guy bursts through the door. He looks mad as fuck. He gets this band out of a box." Adrian lifted his wrist and showed it to Antony.

"That looks like some really cool piece of tech." Antony gazed at the band and its red glow.

"So then this guy pins me against the wall and sticks this band into my wrist. Next thing I know I'm blacked out on the floor. Then I wake up and… I can't control myself. I hit the fat guy really hard, escape the house and fly…"

"Fly?"

"Not anymore. I just have a little spring in my step. Anyway, I just feel really strong."

Antony sighed and leant back in his chair. "I think that's enough drink for one night okay. I think you should get some sleep."

Adrian was getting frustrated. "Antony seriously. You have to believe me when I'm talking about this band. It gives me powers."

He walked over to Antony's bed. He had to prove his point. With one hand he lifted it up from the ground up to his shoulder.

Antony squinted and rubbed his eyes. "Okay I believe you, now please don't destroy my bed. What do you want from me?"

"I know you're quite skilled with the computer stuff. I need to find out what this does and who made it." Adrian showed Antony the etchings on the band.

"I don't know Adrian. It might take some breaking into places and the people who gave you this seem like the kind of people I don't want coming after me."

"Antony please do it. The band is acting up. It's not safe. It's going to kill me."

Antony groaned. "Okay fine. What should I search first?"

"The band says Grapheos."

Antony searched the name. "Nothing."

"What about the company, Trinity Corp.?"

Antony turned back to his laptop and searched Trinity Corp.

"Wait a second they're that medicinal company in Pittsburgh."

Adrian inched closer to the screen. "That's a coincidence. How'd you know that?"

"I used to do some ambassador work for them. They're not capable of anything like this!"

Adrian sighed. "To be honest I don't trust anyone. We should search them and find out more."

Antony nodded. Adrian was right. He could not let his own personal ties affect his decisions. "They distribute and create important medicine and carry out their own research and development to tackle such diseases like Cancer and Alzheimer's. Nothing about any Grapheos project."

Adrian could feel his hands shaking. He needed some luck. "It must be a secret project. Can you get into the company's network? Try and find any documents."

Antony was less anxious. "I have not had enough sleep for this."

"Come off it Antony all you do when you sleep is dream of Alexa."

Antony gave Adrian a gruelling look. He placed his fingers back on the keyboard and began finding ways into the network.

"Shouldn't we… tell the police that we were knocked out and you got kidnapped?"

"I… I'm really not sure." Adrian thought about it for a moment. "Maybe. Do the police deal with that?"

Antony seemed surprisingly calm about the situation much to Adrian's relief. After a few minutes he came across some information.

"Wait I have something." Antony pointed at the screen. "Here, specialist project. It's only mentioned by communications between the owners and the team leader."

"Who's the team leader?"

"His name is Lucas Arkwright. Recognise him?"

"Yeah he's the guy that was running the tests. This special project has to be Grapheos!" Adrian was becoming increasingly optimistic.

"If I go back I can access his whole message string." It seemed the tiredness was no longer present in Antony. It had been replaced with excitement.

Adrian on the other hand, was still agitated. "Anything?"

"One of the first team leader emails is a list of appointed scientists. Do you recognise any of them?"

"No, but I might need to pay one of them a visit. Can you print that out?"

"Sure boss."

"Any information on the product itself?"

"There is absolutely nothing on Grapheos. Almost like it's a secret within a secret. Inception." Antony giggled at his own joke. Adrian just shook his head in disagreement.

"Hang on, there is another scientist who joined a bit later. Rebecca Turnbull." Antony bought up her profile.

Adrian looked closely at the laptop screen. *It could not be could it?* He was horrified at what we was seeing.

"Do you recognise her?" Antony asked as Adrian's stare was fixed on the computer screen.

"Yeah I recognise her… that's my mum."

Weakness

Seven Years Ago. Ella Leones. The proud wife of Peter, a reliable and loving husband. The proud mother of Adrian, an intelligent and insightful son. Recently Ella was out of work. The unstable economic climate meant house prices rose and less people could afford to buy properties. The estate agent company that employed her soon had to reassess their budget. Staff cutbacks were necessary and Ella was one of the first to be made redundant. She considered how she was going to break the news to her family. She felt she had let them down. Ella took a long breath before stepping into her home. She was greeted by a lively Adrian.

"Hey mum, how was work?" He asked as he grabbed a seat on the sofas and turned the TV on.

Mrs Leones brushed off her worries and put on a smile. "The usual, how was school?"

"Same old boring day." Adrian replied.

Ella shrugged at Adrian. "Well that's life." She headed to the kitchen to grab a yogurt from the fridge. Then she returned to the sofas and sat next to Adrian. Adrian's focus shifted away from the TV and onto Ella.

"Do you think there is a reason to why things happen?"

Ella rolled her eyes. She had been here before. "What do you mean?"

"For instance, good luck and bad luck. Karma. Will you making one choice in life have an effect on another?"

Ella moved her mouth to the side as she thought about the question. "That's a tough one. What do you think?"

"I'm not sure. It's comforting to think we have some kind of control."

Ella offered a measured response. "It's only human nature to convince ourselves we control things. That we have a say in the world."

"Maybe the universe does balance things out though, in the end."

Ella smiled. "Maybe son. Maybe."

Adrian and Ella continued to chat for a couple of hours before Peter returned from work.

WEAKNESS

Peter was only around five foot eleven inches in height but to Adrian he always seemed taller. He had a naturally friendly and honest demeanour, reflecting his charming face and short dark curly hair. Ella rose from her seat, hugged him and gave him a kiss on the cheek. Adrian turned around and gave him a simple welcome before returning his gaze to the television.

"There is something we need to talk about." Ella's words sounded guilty. Peter knew something was not right. She led him to the kitchen where Peter poured himself a small glass of whisky, adding ice from the fridge.

Ella stared at him as he took the first sip. "The company isn't doing too well."

Peter lowered his eyebrows in curiosity.

Ella's eyes started to fill with tears. "I've been let go."

Peter moved to comfort her. "Oh no. Don't feel bad it's okay." He hugged Ella. Away from Ella's view, his facial expression changed. He looked worryingly in Adrian's direction.

Later that night, Peter decided to raise the financial issue with Ella. Ella was getting ready for bed whilst he was watching the TV in their bedroom. They had not spoken since they were in the kitchen.

"What do we do about money?" He began.

Ella turned to her husband. "I know I will have to find another job." She slipped into her nightwear. "Can your salary not support us until then?"

Peter looked concerned. He was constantly rubbing his neck and his arm. "It won't. You have to find a job as soon as possible. I'll see what I can do tomorrow."

Ella was surprised by his reaction. "Whoa! We are not in that much trouble." She climbed into bed and faced her husband. "Anyway, finding a job is something I have to do, not you."

"You mean I can't help you. You're my wife, I want to help."

Ella placed her hand on top of Peter's. She noticed it mildly shaking "Peter, we can get through this together. Just relax." She kissed Peter on the cheek, relaxed into the bed and switched her bedside lamp off.

Peter's anxiety was still evident. He switched the television off and tried to fall asleep. But he had no luck. After a few hours of turning and resting, his eyes were still wide open. He slowly crawled out of the bed, gently lifting the sheets so he did not wake Ella. Then he gradually made his way down the stairs towards the kitchen. Peter poured himself another glass of whisky and stared into the night.

* * *

The next day Peter returned from work with important news. He rushed inside the house and headed to the kitchen to talk to Ella. As he opened a can of beer he wanted to make sure Adrian could not hear them talk.

"Where's Adrian?" He asked.

"He's at Erik's today. You look agitated, why don't you sit down?" Ella moved towards him and touched his shoulder.

Peter chose not to listen. He was desperate to get his words out. "There is something I have to tell you."

Ella looked confused. "What is it?"

Peter exhaled. "I found you a job."

"What!? That's great, how? What will I be doing?"

"I spoke to my boss and there is a role for you. I can't talk about the role just yet but it is good trust me. You'll learn all about it at training tomorrow."

Ella was stunned at the news. "That's wonderful." She wrapped her arms around Peter's hips and kissed him. "See I told you everything will be okay. I love you."

Ella was excited to start a new job, even if she was unsure what it would entail. It was a relief for her to start providing income for the family again. Ella was never clear on their financial situation. It was something that Peter would always sort out. If he felt that she needed a job then that was what she had to do. Regardless of whether she enjoyed it or not. After all their years of marriage she trusted his judgement.

The next morning came and both Ella and Peter were up early. They helped Adrian get to school before making their own way to the Pittsburgh Steelers franchise. At least, that was what Ella had been led to believe. But Peter had other ideas. He could see Ella smiling in the passenger seat next to him. He was convinced he was doing the right thing. *I have nothing to worry about.* Ten minutes into the journey he decided it was time.

"There is something you have to know before we get there."

"What is it honey?" Ella smile shone brightly against the morning sun. It made Peter a little more reluctant to say anything.

He calmly took a deep breath and summoned the courage. "I have not been working for the Pittsburgh Steelers."

Ella's smile suddenly switched off. She was bewildered. "What? What are you talking about?"

"In this job, I make more money. You can too." Peter broke a smile. But it did not help.

"What job? I don't understand, what's happening?" Ella's face filled with concern. The worry from the tone of her voice was clear.

Peter stayed calm. "I did this so we could have a better life. You, me and Adrian."

"Did what? Peter, who do you work for?"

"It's a gang called Sinaloa Cartel."

"A gang!? Your job is working for a gang and you only tell me now?" Ella was furious.

Peter was surprised. "It's…"

"It's what Peter, complicated?" Ella's body language was frantic. Her hands were rubbing against her hair. "Oh my god, does that mean you've killed people?"

Peter tried to stay focused on the road. "No, I work in finance."

Ella raised her voice. "Does that make it better? You help fund a group of criminals? Do you know how bad that sounds?"

Peter still spoke quietly, defending himself. "I did it for us Ella."

"No." Ella shook her head. "Do you not realise this puts your family in more danger?"

"They wouldn't harm you. I know that."

"Wait…" Ella's face suddenly froze. "Is that where you're taking me now?"

"I've gotten you work with us Ella."

"No, get me out of this car I am not working for a gang of criminals Peter." Ella's right arm stretched over to the wheel.

"Stop!" Peter shouted.

But her movements were too delirious. She barged into Peter causing the car to swerve into a metal guardrail by the side of the road. Once the rubber from the front tyres made contact, the car flipped into the air. In an instant the car landed upside down and skidded across the surface into a small ditch. Ella lay still above Peter. No movement. Just blood.

* * *

Ella felt her muscles come alive across her body. She had been staring at the afternoon sun through the window for the past few minutes, unable to move. As her lungs filled she closed her eyes and took a deep breath. She used her arms to nudge herself towards the window. Peter was static, still knocked out from the collision. Ella saw this as an opportunity. She gently sprawled across the floor, dragging herself through the window and out of the overturned car. As she gazed back at the wreckage she could feel the true nature of the pain in her limbs. But nothing was broken. She stood, albeit unstably, on her two legs. As she peered over the small ditch they had fallen in she noticed something. There was no one around. The road was clear. There were no passers-by.

Darkness.

Breathless. Ella found herself trying to grapple free from the tight grip that had a hold around her head. Then her instinct kicked in. Running out of breath she kicked her leg backwards, sending herself rolling down the ditch along with the other person. As she turned her head back towards the sun, the shadow of Peter cast upon her. He was holding a pistol to her head.

Ella was astonished. "What are you doing?"

Peter gritted his teeth and stared down at Ella. "We need to move away from here."

Ella pulled herself backwards, ignoring the friction of the gravel below her. "We need to go to a hospital."

"Help is on its way." Peter lowered his gun and offered to help Ella get to her feet.

Ella turned away and picked herself up. "You think a gang of thugs is gonna help us?"

"They're good people."

"You're disillusioned."

"I'm misunderstood." Peter paused. "We are misunderstood."

Ella gave him a smug look. Peter gestured for her to start walking through the empty field.

"Where are you taking me?"

"Somewhere safe. So they can pick us up."

"Won't somebody find the car?"

Peter looked at Ella. "We always have a plan. Just keep walking."

"Why did I choose to marry you?" Ella started to laugh quietly to herself. "Of all the people I could've loved."

Peter brought himself forward to Ella's side. He lifted his arm slightly and grabbed her hand. "Because I'm the only one you truly loved."

Ella moved away from him. "I used to Peter. But you've changed."

"For the better."

"No. For the last few years you've been different. All this now. It makes sense. But why? Why make such a weak decision when you had everything a person could want?"

Peter carried on walking, looking straight ahead. He did not respond. None of what Ella was saying was making him think differently. This was who he really was. Ella stared at him in silence.

Peter put his arm around her to guide her to the long black Mercedes that was waiting. He first helped Ella climb into the back before fitting in next to her. Salazar glanced around the car from the driver's seat. Sat next to Peter was the most beautiful girl he had ever seen. He could not look away,

Peter noticed Salazar staring and decided it was time to introduce him. "These are the guys in the gang."

Ella did not react.

"Darling I'm sorry if you don't agree with my decisions. But you have to know I love you. With all my heart. Everything I do is to protect you and Adrian."

Ella silently wrapped her arms around his hips. She leant onto his chest and whispered the three words he wanted to hear. "I love you."

After fifteen minutes of driving, the group arrived at the gang's main unit. Once she was out the car, Ella eyed up the large factory unit.

"Welcome to my work." Peter smiled.

"Wouldn't the police spot this place?"

"The police haven't been around these parts in decades. Plus, the work I do on the accounts always leads them to dead ends."

"Let me show you inside." Salazar pointed to the small door in the corner and led the group inside. Ella's head began to pound. It had been bandaged in the car but it was still sore.

"Who's that?" Ella whispered as she stuck beside Peter.

"That's Salazar's assistant Simon."

Salazar and Simon led the way as they entered the busy factory. Piled all over the factory floor were packets of white and green substances, out in the open like it was just another product. The back of the factory was a greenhouse, full to the top with cannabis plants. The drugs, the people, the crime. Ella started twitching. Nothing about this made her feel comfortable. Peter took her up to his office where Salazar and Simon joined them. It was time for her to make a decision.

"I should have expected your reaction to all of this." Peter began.

Ella did not respond.

Peter's voice took a solemn tone. "This has been my life for the past few years. I finally get to share it with the woman I love."

Ella spoke quietly "It's going to take time repairing our relationship Peter."

"I know."

She moved closer and placed her hands onto his hips. "But its challenges like this… if anyone can get through it, it's us."

Peter looked down at her. "We'll be stronger for it. So what do you want to do?"

Ella turned around and looked at Salazar. "What exactly will I be doing?"

Salazar stared at her alluring posture. "Mrs Leones you will help us complete orders, avoid the authorities and help our communications with other units in Mexico and various." He broke gently into a smile. "You will become part of our family."

Ella shuddered at the thought.

Simon decided to add more to the selling pitch. "Not to mention your earnings Mrs Leones. A guaranteed exceptional quality of life. And the chance to work alongside your husband."

WEAKNESS

Ella stood silent for a few minutes. This was her chance to get away. But could she? Maybe this was a good offer. Ella nodded her head and looked into Peter's loving eyes.

"I'll do it."

Wait

Ella watched on from her room. Salazar was lying on his death bed. *A death bed he made.* She had not seen him move in the last half-hour. But she did not care. Ella had wished to see this moment from the day she laid eyes on him. With Adrian safe it was like her Christmas had come early. It did not matter what Simon and the others had in store for her.

Simon nervously waited downstairs for any news on Salazar. Lucas was limited in terms of medical equipment to complete a full diagnosis.

"What's the damage?" Simon dared to ask the question.

"I'm afraid it's not good." Lucas looked upon Simon with sympathy. "The collision with the wall has caused significant internal bleeding. He doesn't have long."

Simon laid his left hand on the shoulder of his dying boss. Salazar's eyes started to flicker open. His hand gently raised above his stomach as he groaned in pain.

"Lucas…" Lucas rushed over to Salazar as he woke up.

"Can you hear me?" Lucas asked.

Salazar turned his head towards Lucas. He lightly nodded his head before turning back to Simon. He lifted his hand and placed it on the side of Simon's arm.

"Come closer." Salazar whispered.

Simon looked at Lucas before leaning in to Salazar.

"I know I don't have much time."

"Don't be stupid you're gonna make it."

"No Simon. You have to listen. There is something you must see."

Simon was curious. He leaned in further.

"In my office, the second draw down in my desk. There is a document marked Peter's investigation. It has all the information we have. You need to look at it and show Ella."

"Why did you not tell me about this before?"

"It wouldn't have done you any favours. I had to wait until the time was right."

Simon felt a little insulted.

"Simon, don't let my death be in vain. Carry on… fighting…"

As he uttered his last word his head fall back into the pillow and his eyes closed.

"Sir…, Lucas what's happening?"

Lucas placed his fingertips on his neck and shook his head at Simon. "I'm sorry, he's gone."

"What… Can you not resuscitate him?"

"His heart doesn't have enough blood." Lucas stared sympathetically at Simon. "It wouldn't help. I'm sorry."

Simon looked down on his deceased boss and echoed his last words. "Carry on fighting." Lucas could see the grief he was experiencing.

Simon gritted his teeth. His hands began to tremble. His eyes filled with rage. In an instant he stormed up both flights of stairs before drawing out a gun in point black range from Ella's face.

"He's dead!" He screamed

Ella looked at him, unthreatened. "Good."

The gun was rattling in his grip. "Your son killed him."

"So," Ella paused. "What are you waiting for?"

Lucas and Malcolm rushed into the room. "Stop, Simon don't do this." Lucas shouted.

"Stay out of this. Or you'll be next."

"This isn't what you want. It won't fix anything." Lucas urged. "It won't bring him back."

"I have no use for any of you. And he isn't here to save you. So why shouldn't I shoot you all?"

"Because you won't," Ella replied.

Simon kept the pistol pointing at her head.

"Because the person you really have to go after is Adrian!" Lucas blurted.

Simon turned his head towards Lucas.

"And you won't be able to beat him without our help." Lucas continued.

Simon lowered his gun. He looked at Ella deep in the eyes.

"I'm not going to kill you. That can wait." He started grinning. "But first I want to see your face when I slice your son's throat."

Simon began to walk away but Ella wanted the last word. "You won't kill him. You can't."

Simon stopped. Her self-assured attitude was irritating him. It was time for her to face her demons. "You have so much pride in your family don't you? Adrian the prodigal son, Peter the hard working husband."

Ella shrugged. "It's fair to say they've made mistakes, but they're not bad people."

Simon laughed. "Not bad people? Peter worked for us! You and he have helped us kill."

"He cared about his family."

"You don't know do you?" Simon continued to laugh.

"Know what?" Ella dropped her eyebrows.

"All this time, he never told you."

"Told me what?"

"The real reason he came to work for us."

"That greedy bastard wanted more money." Ella responded.

"Oh no. No… No… No…" Simon was still smiling. He was enjoying this. "Your lovely husband Peter. He did work for the Pittsburgh Steelers. What a job that was. Good money too. But he just could not keep away his addictions."

"What do you mean?"

"You never noticed? His alcohol addiction. He once got to work four hours late smelling of the stuff. But the reason he was late was because the police caught up with him. He was fired on the spot, couldn't find another job. Ran out of money. Didn't want to tell you about it."

"You're lying."

"You're telling me you never saw him without a drink?"

Ella recalled her moments with Peter.

"He came to us for a loan. But he couldn't pay it. So we offered him the chance to work with us. Pay off his debt that way. We were never comfortable when you came into the equation. But we ignored it because business was doing so well… we got complacent."

"No he would tell me about that."

Ella naturally dismissed Simon's suggestion. But an overriding part of her knew it was the truth she had been hiding from her whole life.

"Would he really?"

The question lingered over Ella's head. Her heart said yes. Her mind said no.

"Why did you take him?"

Simon chuckled again. "We didn't! Why would we take away the man that gave us the success we only dreamed about?"

"Because he became a threat. Along with me we were going to expose all this!"

"Nonsense. We gave him a home when all was lost. You just can't face the fact that he enjoyed working for us!"

"That's not true!"

Simon looked at Ella for a minute. He had a plan. He headed to Salazar's office, barged through the door and flung open the second desk draw. Inside was just a pile of papers. Simon started rummaging through them knocking everything onto the floor. Then he found what he was looking for. *Peter's Investigation.* Simon pulled out the file and placed it on the desk in front of him. He carefully read each paragraph and studied each photograph as he flicked through the short folder. The file told a story of its own. His next move was crucial.

Simon rushed out of the office and gathered everyone together.

"Everybody listen up! We need guns and ammo, bombs and whatever else we can find. I want that women tied up. Don't let her out of your sight." He paused and lowered his voice. "We're going on a little trip."

The Sinaloa gunmen dispersed. Lucas brought himself towards Simon.

"Lucas, I need to ask you some questions." The two disappeared into Salazar's old office.

"So, how can we stop Adrian?" Simon asked.

"Well I thought a bullet through his head but he was clearly too powerful for that."

"I don't want to hear that. Is there another way?"

"Taking off the band will make him vulnerable for sure. It might even kill him. But how will you find him?"

Simon pondered the question. "You're telling me that band doesn't have a tracker?"

Lucas trembled. "Of course. My apologies."

Simon smiled. It was time for the final rallying cry. "He will come to us. And we will have our revenge!"

Come Home

Antony had managed to persuade Adrian to get some sleep before making his journey home. He stayed the rest of the night and the next day at college. But Adrian slept through all of it. Through all the hallway conversations, the visit by the accommodation team to fix Antony's window smashed by 'youths' and the phone calls he was receiving every hour. His friends were evidently worried. The band still locked onto his wrist had not caused him any pain. It seemed when his movements were static the band mirrored his rest. Adrian was sat at the end of his bed. For the first time in a while he felt well rested. He could see the sunset leak through the closed blinds, hitting his face in parallel lines. Adrian planned on facing his mother at his home in Pittsburgh. He wanted to know more about the band on his wrist and why she had lied to him about her real job. Adrian had never spoken to his mother in a direct tone but he wanted answers.

There was no point in waiting anymore. Adrian knew the time had come to set off.

Antony told him to wait until the next morning, claiming a storm was predicted that could delay the trains. But the weather had been perfect. The train was his only route home for a surprise visit. He wondered how his mother would react to seeing him. *Would she even be home?* Adrian took a quick shower and slipped on grey chinos, a plain red t-shirt and thin black leather jacket. There was one last thing he needed. From the inside of his bottom draw, he pulled out his diary and placed it in his jacket. Adrian knew he ran the risk of being recognised by any of the thugs he saw. He was certain they would be actively trying to track him down and get the band back. *Why haven't they come to the place I live?* It was a question that concerned Adrian particularly as he had another home. And he intended on going straight there.

Adrian first had to make sure that no one in the flat would see him leave. He carefully inched closer to his door and placed his ear in the small gap between the doorway and the door. He could not hear anything. He peered through the eye glass, looking edge to edge. No one was around. Gently pushing down the door handle, he pulled his door open just enough to squeeze through. Once he was in the hallway he held onto the door so it could shut without making a sound. He tiptoed across and made it through the flat door unnoticed. As he left the building he pulled his hood up. They would not recognise him if they could not see his whole face. He headed towards the bus stop and waited.

Soon he arrived at New York's grandest train station, Grand Central. It was one of the most iconic stations in the world. The large open area in the centre was packed with hundreds of travellers. Two enveloping sets of stairs at each side lead the way to shops and restaurants. Adrian approached the ticket counter and purchased a ticket to Pittsburgh. The ticket man was direct and cold, reflective of Adrian's mission. As he headed to the platform, a policeman tapped him on the shoulder.

"Excuse me sir, can you please take your hood down?"

Adrian quickly turned around to see the large officer. He first glanced at the gun in his holster before looking up.

Adrian lowered his hood and apologised. "Sorry officer."

He continued walking to his platform, number 4.

* * *

During the train journey Adrian did a lot of thinking. He rehearsed the questions he was going to ask and was trying to predict how his mother would react. He wondered what the best case scenario would be and how the night could end in the worst case scenario. It was a chilling thought. This was the perfect moment for reflection since this was the first time he was returning home since he moved out. Adrian took his diary out from inside his jacket and penned another entry.

27/05/2015

Back home, back to the place where I experienced some of the worst times in my personal life. I don't like using the mirrors there. They take me back to the times when I used to hate myself. I used to be angry at the person staring back. People might call me special. But I don't see it that way. I'm not happy with the way I am. It's all brought on by nature, I did not cause this. It's in my genes. I have to make sure I don't go down that path again, hating myself for it. That's why it's so important that mentally, I'm perfect. My brain lifted me out of the ground when I was six feet under, it teaches me to never give up and no matter how bad things get, to just keep going. The small moments, words and pictures make me realise I'm too insignificant to care about my own problems. That has been my coping mechanism. It keeps me focused and true to the heart. Hopefully one day I can take a chance to show people what I can really do and show them what sets me apart.

- Adrian

Being at home reminded Adrian of troubling times. It was easy to escape these when he was at college. But now he had to face his troubles head on. It was more important than ever to keep his head and pull through.

The train had reached its destination. As Adrian stepped foot inside Pittsburgh he felt the heavy rain pour down onto him. *Antony was right.* The weather was enough to put Adrian off walking home, instead opting for a taxi. The driver was silent. Adrian was silent. There was too much on his mind for small talk. He chose to stare blankly at the rain hitting the streets of his home town.

Then the taxi pulled up outside his house. Just as it did two and a half years ago. He was about to face his mother again.

Adrian paid his fare and stepped out the car. The rain was still hurtling down from the heavens. He walked up to the front door and gently angled the door slightly open to peer inside. All he could see was darkness. He checked his watch. 11:23pm. His mother was probably asleep by now. Adrian took a step inside the house and quietly closed the door behind him. He decided to call his mother.

After a couple of shouts he heard a door creak open upstairs. Adrian stayed by the stairs and stared up into the blackness. Then the hallway light flickered into life. Adrian stared intently to see who or what was going to emerge. It was his mother. Her clothes were worn and dirty and Adrian could see cuts and bruises on her face, arms and legs. Once she laid eyes on Adrian her face turned to shock and horror. Her mouth was wide open as she placed the palm of her hand on top.

"Adrian." She whispered to herself. Then she leapt down the stairs and wrapped her arms around the stunned young man. Adrian stayed still, not quite knowing what was happening. After a few moments Ella let go and faced her son.

"I'm so happy to see you! C'mon we have to go."

"Go?" Adrian replied.

Ella opened the door behind Adrian. Adrian immediately reacted and slammed the door shut with all his energy. The loud crash made Ella back away from him.

"I'm sorry. But we're not going anywhere. I have a lot of questions."

"Adrian, what do you know?" Ella looked concerned.

"I know you lied to me about your job."

"Honey, what happened to your hand?" Ella spotted the band on Adrian's wrist. The skin around it was burnt and his veins were raised.

"You should know. This is something you have worked on!"

"Adrian I'm sorry, I didn't mean for it to be used that way."

Adrian did not have time for her apologies. "Why did you lie to me?"

"I had to Adrian. To keep you safe."

"Keep me safe from what? All you have done is give me a reason not to trust you!"

Ella held onto Adrian's arm. "I had to save you from the real world."

Adrian instantly brushed her off. "What? You mean the real world where a gang of men kidnap and try to kill me?"

Ella's voice suddenly changed. "You just had to be the hero didn't you?" It no longer sounded caring but fierce and intense.

Adrian was overwhelmed. "What?"

"If you didn't put yourself out there in school nobody would even know you existed."

"I did what I could to protect the people around me. More than what you can say."

"Your father and I did what we had to for you."

"You don't understand it do you? How does lying to your own child sound right?"

"Me and your father made mistakes. I'll admit that." Ella paused. "Where do you want to go from here?"

"What is this?" Adrian lifted his arm and showed his mother the band. "What is the special project?"

Ella sighed. "Trinity did a lot of good things. But what nobody knew about was our hidden intentions. The owners wanted to find a way of moving humanity forward. By fusing normal people with pure energy."

Adrian shook his head. "Do you know how stupid that sounds?"

"I was never comfortable with it. But the owners were insistent that I worked on it." Ella hesitated. "They said I would lose my job."

Adrian showed no sympathy by deciding to ask another question "Who is Lucas?"

"Lucas was the team leader for the project. He believed in the project and after it started to fail, he escaped and went rogue."

"How do you know that?"

"He asked if I would join him. I said no."

"Liar. The police would be after you."

"If the police were after me then how am I still here? Adrian that band is dangerous. It was never intended for use. We have to get it off you."

"How? This was your friend Lucas' fault you know?"

"It wasn't Lucas that put it on you." Ella quickly stopped and gasped.

Adrian's face was stunned. "How do you know it wasn't Lucas?"

Ella stared deeply into Adrian's eyes. She just made a costly mistake.

In The Middle

Waiting. Anticipating. This operation was the first of its kind that the gang have experienced. They have been through shoot outs, robbery and murders but not this. Not trapping a man who has abilities beyond a normal human. Of all the missions for Simon to lead for the first time it had to be this one. His head and his heart was full of rage. His grief was being displayed in pure anger for the man he was staring at. Simon had to get his revenge. He had watched Adrian enter the house and speak to his mother. It was a risk to let her loose and he knew she would try to escape. But Adrian had other ideas. He had questions that needed answering. He was not going to let her go anywhere.

Simon wanted to go out there right now and exact his revenge. But he had to be patient. He had his gang surrounding the house and ready to burst through the front and back doors. Simon was watching on from a small monitor placed in Ella's room. It not only showed Ella and Adrian but also cameras placed on a few of the thugs. The image of Salazar's dead body was still engraved on his mind. Simon was taken back to his times as a teenager. He remembered how Salazar trained him and offered him guidance. Salazar taught him a lot. It all started the day he joined the gang.

Simon and his family lived in a small flat in Bushwick, Brooklyn, New York. His mother was a hair dresser and his father was unemployed. He made the family live off small-time government benefits. He also had a younger sister who was soon moving onto high school. Simon's parents never cared about him. The only time they spoke to him was when he got into trouble at school. That was quite often. Simon was not brought up with any morals. He had no reason to care about anyone else but himself. He resented the privileged children. *What made them so deserving of a lucky life?* One evening Simon was out looking for trouble. He wanted cash, a phone or anything with any value. It was a dark and rainy day. Simon strolled through the streets in a black coat with a hood on top of his head. Below his coat he held a long and sharp knife. He arrived at a street which usually had a few visitors every night. He decided to stop and lean against the shutters of shop. Waiting. Anticipating. As he glanced to his right a gang of around four people started to close in on him quickly. They were each wearing balaclavas and carrying handguns. Simon did not fear them. He had nothing they could take. One of the men raised their gun at Simon. He slowly lifted up his hands and dropped the knife out of his hand. Another of the men pulled down Simon's hood and then searched him for anything he could find.

Simon stared at the eyes of another member of the gang. It was time to make his move. With his left leg he kicked the face of the man searching his trousers. Then he knocked the handgun out of the thug's hand before swinging his fist towards a third member and knocking him to the floor. Anticipating a reaction from the others, Simon threw himself to the floor and rolled away from all the action. He then arose, pointing a gun in the direction of the two remaining men standing. One of the men pulled off his mask. It was a younger, slimmer Salazar. He stared at Simon and smiled.

"My child, that was excellent. But you still have a lot to learn." Salazar looked down to Simon's hip.

Confused, Simon glanced below to see blood pouring out of his hip. A knife had penetrated his skin. He pulled it out, fell to the floor and let out a cry in agony.

"What are you waiting for? Help him!" Salazar said to the men on the floor. They quickly scampered up and put Simon on his back. They worked to stop the bleeding and stitched up the wound. This was the first time Simon had been cared for. It was also the first time somebody had complemented him for his skills but pointed out the need for improvement. Salazar leaned down to talk to him.

"You have great skills my friend. Where did you learn?"

"It's just reaction. Growing up here, I needed it." Simon answered.

"That is not just reaction. That is natural skill. How would you like to join us?"

"Us? Who are you?"

"I come from Mexico, from the gang Sinaloa Cartel."

"I've heard about them. They make a lot of money."

"And you can be a part of it." Salazar offered his hand to help Simon stand up. He took a few minutes to think about his offer. But the answer was clear to him. He grabbed Salazar's hand and faced him eye to eye.

"I know just the place we can start." Simon and Salazar both smiled.

Salazar was the first person to look after Simon. Under his guidance he became one of the best members of the gang and was soon given the chance in a senior role. It was a role he thrived under, becoming the closest advisor to Salazar. But now his boss was dead. It was up to Simon to keep the remaining members in New York functioning. But he had to avenge Salazar's death. Salazar did not die by the hand of this kid for nothing. He was not going to get away with it. Not while Simon and his team were still breathing.

A voice grabbed Simon's attention. "The cars are ready sir."

Simon nodded. He was going to have his revenge.

* * *

Ella and Adrian stared at each other in silence. The truth of the matter was slowly dawning on Adrian. Ella was speechless.

"Were you there?" Adrian's voice got louder. He was outraged. The band on his wrist started to glow brighter.

Ella inched away from her son. "Adrian I'm sorry."

"ANSWER ME!"

Just as Adrian raised his voice further two men burst through the front door and knocked Adrian onto the ground. A second wave of men emerged from the kitchen area, grabbing Ella and directing their weapons towards the young man. Adrian could feel the band working again. With a powerful shove he pushed both the men off his back and sent them crashing into the wall. Adrian stood tall off the ground. His eyes lit up with a familiar deep red. The other men were hesitant to move. They were in awe of the effect the Grapheos was having. But there was a problem. The band stuttered and Adrian fell to the ground in excruciating pain. The men watched on as the man they feared moments ago was no longer able to stand.

"For fuck sake pick him up and get him in the car!" Simon emerged from the stairs and started shouting at his team. It seemed to wake them up. They grabbed Ella, picked Adrian up and threw them into the back of a car waiting outside. As the dust settled inside the house the full scale of destruction could be seen. Glass covered the blood-stained floor and the side wall looked like it was about to fall apart. It no longer looked like a family home. It was a crime scene.

Ella sat still opposite an unconscious Adrian in a mini-van. Alongside her was Lucas and Simon. Next to Adrian was Malcolm and an armed gangster. Lucas moved across to assess Adrian. The band was stuttering but his pulse was still beating. As Lucas assessed Adrian's wrist Ella tried to convince them to leave him alone.

"You can't take it off."

Lucas looked at Simon who turned to Ella.

"We have to." Simon replied.

Ella became frantic. "You'll kill him."

"That wouldn't be so bad will it?" Simon grinned.

Ella felt her stomach churn. She stared at Simon for a moment before spitting in his face. Simon flinched and wiped away the saliva from his cheek. He started chuckling again. Then he clenched his fist and punched Ella square in the face. Her upper body dropped onto her seat. Ella moaned in pain as she clenched her face. Malcolm and Lucas watched in silence.

"Take it off." Simon ordered Lucas.

Ella picked herself back up and wiped away the fresh blood on her mouth. Lucas placed Adrian's arm on his lap. Then he found the two ends of the band that were fixed into his veins. He looked towards Simon for further confirmation. Simon nodded. Lucas grabbed one end of the band and with a mighty push he tore it away from Adrian's skin. Blood started to pour from his wrist. Ella winced and turned away. Tears mounted underneath her eyes. Lucas quickly pulled out the other end and bandaged Adrian's wrist, pushing tight to stop the bleeding. Adrian's body started to violently shake as his body reacted to the sudden withdrawal of the substance. Lucas pulled away from him until he stopped and relaxed back into his seat. Lucas checked Adrian's pulse. Ella peered nervously towards her son as she waited for Lucas to speak. Adrian's life could have reached its end.

Turn Around

"There you go all done. We'll be on our way now."

It had been just six hours since Adrian smashed Antony's bedroom window and discovered his mother's secret life. Two middle-aged builders had been sent by the accommodation office to replace the window.

"Great thanks."

Antony closed the door behind the builders and looked outside his new window. It had been an overcast night. The clouds seemed to be preparing for a storm late last night. Antony had warned Adrian against any travelling. It was too risky. It was too dangerous. The events of the previous night had been playing on his mind. *Adrian is kidnapped and then gets powers.* It could have easily been a bad dream but he woke up hugging his covers for warmth. The smashed window had sent a refreshingly cold breeze into his room all night. *After Adrian wakes up, then we can get answers.* Antony had assumed Adrian knew just as much as he did about the situation. But Adrian was suspiciously casual about everything.

Antony remembered why they were out in the first place. Jayden wanted to cheer him up about Alexa being with someone else. Antony felt like such a fool. He risked a friendship for nothing. Maybe it was time for him to tell her the truth and get it off his mind. It seemed like the only way. Antony put on a red baseball style jacket and white converse trainers and headed to the kitchen to see if anyone was in there. There was no sign of Adrian but Jayden was there once again, sat at the table eating a sandwich and playing on his iPad.

"Hey man, how's your window?"

"It's cool, some guys came in and replaced it. It's like new now."

"I still can't believe someone would do that. It's so random. Tom and that other girl from next door flat, what's her name…?"

"Charice?"

"Yeah. They came round to see what happened. They said it woke them all up."

"I think it woke the whole neighbourhood up. Anyway, it's done and it's fixed. I think we can all move on."

"You could have been injured though. What if a piece of glass hit you in the face or the eye?"

Antony rolled his eyes. "I don't like to think about it like that. It didn't and I just want to move on. Speaking of moving on guess where I'm going?"

"Somewhere where they give advice to fully grown adults about dealing with kids that are bullying them?" Jayden smiled.

"That's hilarious," Antony sarcastically replied. "I'm actually off to tell Alexa the truth and then I'm moving on."

"Aw nice can I join you for a drink after?" Jayden asked.

"Yeah sure."

"And Adrian?"

"If he's awake." Antony smiled and walked towards the door. But just before he left Jayden had a few more words for his friend.

"Before you go, I think you're doing the right thing. You've made some pretty stupid decisions before. But this is the right one."

"Thanks Jay."

Antony made the short walk to Alexa's flat. The walkway was still dry but the clouds above had darkened. He pulled out his phone and gave Alexa a call. After a couple of minutes he could see her light brown boots descend the stairs. A dress with light blue and black patterns followed, before his eyes were drawn to a long beaded wooden necklace close to her chest. She looked like she was about to go somewhere.

"What's up?"

Antony had forgotten how gorgeous she was. He had to concentrate.

"Nothing much…" He stuttered. "It's been a while. How have you been?"

The two continued their small talk as they climbed the two flights of stairs to Alexa's flat.

"What are you doing today?" Alexa asked.

"I haven't got anything planned. Why?"

"Well me and Katy were about to go shopping and get a bite to eat. You can tag along if you need to talk."

"I'm not doing anything else."

Katy arrived a couple of minutes later. Antony knew Katy well from the time he spent with Alexa. She had a similar personality to her, an attractive blonde but smart enough to be independent. The guys would practically queue up. Katy sported a short denim skirt and glamourous heels to show off her legs in the most desirable fashion. A baby blue top and white bracelet finished her outfit off. Antony felt Katy knew how he truly felt about Alexa but it appeared as though Katy had restrained from sharing her opinion. But quite like his relationship with Alexa, this was all guesswork.

"Antony?" Katy hugged Alexa before looking surprised to see him. "I heard about your window. Is everything okay?"

"Oh yeah I heard about that!" Alexa added.

"Everything is fine. Just some silly kids put a brick through it!"

"That's so bad. What did the police say?" Alexa asked.

"I didn't see them do it so it would be really hard to find out who it was."

"There might have been witnesses." Katy raised her eyebrows.

"I don't know who is walking the streets at that time of night!" Antony chuckled.

Katy giggled and looked at Alexa. "You'd be surprised!" Alexa looked back at Katy and gave her a slight nudge.

"What's that about?" Antony asked.

"Nothing." Alexa was quick to change the conversation. "So how's Adrian? I text him last night but haven't heard back."

Antony was confused but he carried on with the conversation. "Adrian stayed up last night. And I don't know why… But at the moment he's sleeping."

"Uh I hate it when that happens." Katy responded.

Alexa sighed. "Yeah I get a messed up sleeping pattern for weeks."

"Oh cool it's a normal thing then." Antony grinned. "I thought Adrian had just gone crazy."

* * *

Alexa, Antony and Katy visited several stores in the New York shopping district, much to Antony's dismay. They stopped for dinner and returned to college in a trip that took them three and a half hours. Katy left during the bus journey leaving Antony alone with Alexa.

The setting sun marked the end of the day. It was time for Antony to have his talk. Just before Alexa entered her flat building, his mouth twitched.

"Alexa, I need to talk to you about something."

Her hair waved back as her innocent expression turned to him. "What is it?"

"You have to understand. I need to get this off my chest." Antony kept his trembling hands close to his chest. He took an unsettling breath before whispering, "I like… like you."

Alexa's expression turned from confusion to realisation. "Oh Antony."

"I would ask if you wanted to go for a drink but I know you're seeing someone."

"Antony I'm sorry." Alexa fell into a sombre mood. "It must be hard to see your best friend with me."

Antony shook his head. "Best friend?"

"You know its Adrian I'm seeing now don't you? He asked me out a few weeks ago."

"ADRIAN!?" Antony screamed. "Fucking bastard hasn't said anything!"

Alexa shifted her eyes. "This isn't good?"

"That manipulative arsehole!"

"Manipulative?"

"He shouted at me for spending too much time with you." Antony gritted his teeth. "Now I know why."

"He shouted at you?"

"That bastard just wanted you all to himself."

Alexa pushed Antony away from her. "I'm not some piece of meat that you and Adrian can fight over!"

"No Alexa it's not like that." Antony held out his hands. "I think we should talk to him."

"I'm not involved in this. This is your problem to deal with."

"But Alexa!"

"I'm sorry that it's turned out this way Antony. I don't even know if I want to be serious with Adrian anymore. But you have to sort your friendship out."

Alexa turned away and scampered inside the building and up the stairs. Antony was left isolated to reflect. The story was bigger than he thought. Telling the truth had added more tension to his head. He had to talk to Adrian. Antony ran back to his flat and stopped facing Adrian's door. He knocked hard on it three times. No answer. He tried again, this time louder. Still nothing.

"Adrian if you're inside please open the door. We need to talk." Antony still received no answer from inside. *What if something has happened to him?* It was possible the band he was wearing may have had a dramatic effect. He could be unconscious. *He could be dead.* Antony's anger soon turned to desperation. He was not taking any chances. He called the accommodation office and asked for someone to come and open the door in a desperate plea. Ten minutes later a man wearing campus security uniform arrived at their flat with a special key card. He unlocked the door to Adrian's bedroom and ran in alongside Antony. They first checked his bed. Nothing. There was nobody in the room. Adrian had gone.

Antony knew. His friend was in danger.

Demons

"He's still breathing."

Ella drew a breath of relief. For now at least Adrian was alive.

After a few minutes he awoke dazed and confused. He sat up right and glanced around at his surroundings. He could feel a sharp pain through his bandaged wrist.

"What happened? Where's the band?" He asked.

Ella reached out and held his hand. Adrian held onto it tightly and looked into her eyes. "What happened to your eye?"

"It's nothing dear." Ella replied.

"The band is not yours Adrian. My boss made a mistake." Simon could not look at Adrian without feeling angry.

"Where is he?" Adrian questioned.

"You killed him."

Adrian could not help but grin. *Finally some good news.*

Simon's anger widened. "It's not funny. Stop smiling or I'll reconsider keeping you alive."

Adrian stopped grinning. He knew he was going to end up dead anyway. But Simon could make it much worse for him.

"Where are you taking us?" Ella's attention switched away from Adrian.

"Good question. Before he died, Salazar set some members of the gang a task. To do some digging into your husband's disappearance."

"Are you trying to make it sound like your innocent in this?"

"You must believe me when I say. We are innocent." Simon shook his head. "Right now, we are on our way to the place where we believe he is. Based on information we have obtained."

"You expect me to believe that you 'obtained' this information?"

"We just thought you would want to see him before you die. Whether you believe us or not, I don't care anymore."

Ella grunted and turned away from Simon. She knew if they did not tell the truth now they never would. It was no longer worth her time.

"We're here." The voice came from the front of the mini-van.

THE FRONT

Simon was out of the car first. His gang gathered Ella and Adrian together to tie their hands around their back. The heavens had opened and the rain was pouring down heavily. A storm was brewing in the clouds. It suddenly got a lot darker. As the whole team followed Simon, Ella bumped into Malcolm. He gave her a nasty look so she backed away. After a short walk, the gang arrived at the scene.

Ahead of them was a large white warehouse covered in graffiti markings, from peculiar names like 'Skeam' to compass directions. It appeared the area had been left abandoned like the car lying in front of it. A Vauxhall Astra in blue. In the middle of nowhere. Its paintwork had rusted away and its tyres had sunk halfway into the ground. Ella recognised it straight away. It was Peter's car that was never found or recovered. The warehouse was familiar to all those in the Sinaloa gang. It was their former headquarters before their dramatic fall. Across from the warehouse was a forest. Simon led the team into the trees. Adrian's physical weakness resulted in a very slow walking pace, sometimes unable to stand. He was being dragged and poked through the mud by two goons watching over him. As they approached a gap in the trees Simon stopped. Ella broke away from the group and ran to the grave in front of him, marked with a bronze cross stuck in the ground. Adrian and the rest of the gang gathered around it. Ella burst into tears and fell to her knees above her late husband.

"This is what we found. That is Peter's car. After some digging, we found his corpse." Simon relaxed his posture. "He's dead Ella."

Ella said nothing. Her tears were her words. Simon cut her hands free from the rope. She brought her arms forward and picked up a handful of soil. For a moment she gazed upon it and held it tight. She felt as if she was holding on to the man she had been missing for the past five years. Ella turned back, tears still streaming from her eyes, and faced Adrian. Adrian struggled to hold in his emotions any longer as he stared at his distraught mother. He ran forwards and buried himself into her arms. The two shared their closest moment together. After a few moments, Ella turned back to Simon.

"Why did you do this?" She questioned.

"We're just showing you what we found." Simon rolled his eyes. "It's amazing isn't it? How much of an effect one family can have. I wonder how many people wanted him dead."

"He was ten times the man you will ever be."

Simon laughed. "And yet there he lies. Able to do nothing about his own family's impending death."

Malcolm looked across at the group and then watched Ella. For a split-second, she turned to him and nodded. It was the indication he had been waiting for. Malcolm pulled out two handguns from his pocket, instantly flinging one towards Ella and using the other to shoot the goon closest to him. Ella managed to grab the flying handgun and adjust her position to face the gang. She shot both the confused gangsters next to Simon whose hesitation had cost them their lives. As they dropped to the floor Malcolm and Ella pointed their guns at an unarmed Simon and Lucas, isolated facing the grave. Ella wiped away more tears.

A composed Simon chuckled quietly. "It looks like I made another bad decision." He gave Malcolm a long and uncomforting stare.

* * *

On the outskirts of Pittsburgh the rain continued to provide an onslaught of attack to the ground below. It showed no signs of receding. Adrian watched on as his mother held a gun to a man he had only just met. Below his knees was his father's grave. A stark reminder of the last five years he had spent without his presence. Adrian did not want to hear anything that was being said. He simply closed his eyes and prayed that he would wake up back in his bed at home. But that was miles away. Adrian had to face his demons.

"You haven't won Ella." Simon continued. "Your husband's dead. His killer will still be out there. He might even target your son." His volume had raised slightly but he was still calm and collected.

"Don't even go there. You, Salazar. Every one of you are the same." Ella gritted her teeth. "Cold hearted killers."

"So kill me then." Simon showed no fear or sympathy for her. "That's the fix!" Simon raised his voice.

Ella trembled as she held the gun at his forehead. She desperately wanted to pull the trigger but instead she lowered the gun.

"You know. All this time you've been pretending. Blaming us. But you knew it wasn't us." Simon smirked. "You can't handle the unknown so you blamed us. It was an easy answer."

Ella turned her attention to Lucas who had been silent the whole time. "What have you got to say?"

"Ella please." Lucas pleaded. "I have nothing to do with them you know that."

"Oh no. You just stood there and did whatever they told you to."

Lucas held his hands out. "I didn't put that band on your son."

Ella quietly laughed. "At what point did you try to save me Lucas?"

"Ella I'm sorry."

Ella put her hand on Luca's shoulder and pushed him down. "Get on your knees."

She looked at Simon "You as well."

The mud and water squeezed beneath them as they hit the ground.

Adrian had his hands over his ears. The shouting in front of him passed through his mind. The dark clouds began to gather above him. The trees surrounded him. Only the grave of his murdered father remained. It haunted him. A dead heartbeat. Beating. Again and again. Adrian could no longer take it.

"Stop!" He shouted. Ella turned around instantaneously. Adrian was on his knees. Tears rolled down his face. He lifted his hands off his ears and laid them down on the ground.

"Stop." He shouted again. "It was me!"

The group stared at Adrian.

"Adrian what are you saying?" Ella's body was numb.

"I'm sorry mum." The tears trickled down Adrian's face as he looked deep into his mother's eyes. "I killed him."

Each word felt like a dagger to her heart. She was lost for words. The gun lay low in palm of her hand, no longer directed at Simon. Malcolm though managed to keep his gun raised towards him.

"Adrian." Ella stated trembling. She moved closer to him. "It was you?"

Adrian could barely see through his tears. He shook his head and looked towards Ella. "I'm sorry."

Ella was now only a foot away from Adrian, on the other side of her husband's grave. She crouched down to his level and stared at her son's face. His words had started to resonate with her.

"After all these years?" Adrian could see the anger in his mother's eyes. Her tears had stopped and her face turned malevolent. Adrian tried to back away a couple of inches but the mud was tough to get through. He sensed danger. His mother was still holding a gun.

In an instant, Ella threw herself towards Adrian and pinned him to the ground. Her left hand clenched. With brutal force she hit Adrian in his face. Adrian reacted quickly and pushed her onto the ground. Both of them rose at the same time and began to grapple control of the other. Adrian spotted the gun in Ella's hand and strained to get hold of it. But in the midst of the chaos, the gun was fired. For a moment, the rain stopped. The noise stopped.

Time stood still.

Adrian could not feel any pain. He glanced below and saw no blood. But then he looked forward. His mother was staring at him, her eyes and mouth wide open. Blood dripped down from her tongue and rolled off her lips. Adrian could see the hole in her chest. The bullet had pierced through her clothes and ripped open her heart. Adrian leapt forward to his mother's aid. She fell to the ground holding on to the last remains of her life. Adrian was the only one surrounding her. She did not speak. She suffered for only a minute until her head fell to the side. Her brain switched off. Adrian felt her pulse but it was in vain. There was no beat. His father lay below him. His mother lay next to him. And all he could do was mourn.

Simon, Malcolm and Lucas watched on in silence. Simon did not try and escape. He was both fascinated and shocked by the turn of events. He almost wanted to give Adrian a handshake. He had everyone fooled including himself. As the atmosphere calmed, flashing red and blue lights lit up the darkness and revealed the pouring rain once again. One police car turned up at the warehouse and policemen on foot surrounded the area around the grave. Hanging in the air above them was a police helicopter. Adrian looked up and felt he was staring at the hand of god bringing an end to the madness. Simon swiftly attempted an escape. He ran into the trees but bumped straight into an officer pointing an automatic weapon to his fallen body. The police officers moved in and handcuffed Lucas, Malcolm and Adrian. There was talking and shouting but Adrian did not hear any of it. As he was dragged away all he could stare at was his fallen mother. Helpless and gone. He kicked, screamed and begged to be back at her side.

As he was pushed into the back of a police car he was left to glance around at the destruction he had caused. His father's beaten and bruised car, his mother being wheeled into the back of an ambulance. His own blood stained body. They were the mark of the wonderful turmoil he created. The images that would stay in his mind forever.

Life in Colour

Adrian was stood in a small box next to the judge at the far end of the large courtroom. It had been a week since his gruesome encounter with the truth. He had not said a word since. The scene still haunted him, flickering through his mind. The judge was sat high above everyone else. The audience were seated on two sides, separated by the walkway to the door. In front of both sides was a place for the accusers and the defenders. But there was no defence. This was simply a sentencing task. All the evidence would be brought up and scrutinised. Adrian will be questioned and a story will be built.

This was the first time Adrian could find no support. He could see no family. He could see no friends. Antony and Alexa had made the effort to travel down to Pittsburgh and see him. But they did not want to support or sympathise with him. Instead they sat hand in hand and represented what he had lost. Adrian stared back, emotionless. Speechless. Until the first lawyer stood up. He was a short Asian male wearing a black suit and polished shoes. He stood confidently in front of the judge and the on looking public. With a strut that made Adrian cringe he approached the young man.

"What is your name?" The man spoke with a strong British accent.

Adrian looked down at his own navy-coloured suit before looking back at the lawyer. He felt like it was a stupid question. He leaned forward towards the microphone.

"Adrian Leones, sir."

The lawyer nodded and proceeded to ask more questions.

"You are charged with the murder to the first degree of your father Peter Leones. How do you plead?"

Adrian shuffled in his place. He glanced at the public awaiting his next words. "Guilty." Nobody reacted.

"You are charged with involuntary manslaughter leading to the death of your mother Ella Leones. How do you plead?"

"Guilty." The word hung in the atmosphere of the courtroom. The lawyer turned back to his colleagues on the desk behind him. He nodded and turned back to Adrian.

"Why would you commit such merciless crimes against your own family?" The audience drew breath. They were about to get the answer to question they all wanted to ask.

Adrian kept a neutral expression. Inside he gritted his teeth. "It was not my intention to... cause such harm." He began. "Can you imagine being a... still a child raised in a loving family. Only to find out it's all lies. To find out that the people you once looked up to, are causing more harm in the world than good. For whatever I did in the future, I would only be making right the things my parents made wrong. At the time, I believed it was for the greater good."

"Do you still believe you did the right thing?"

"It doesn't matter does it?" Adrian replied in a low, soft tone. "What I can say is this. If I was in the same situation now, then I wouldn't have killed my father."

"Are you saying you regret your actions Mr Leones?"

"You don't understand my words Mr... whoever you are. I cannot take back decisions made in the past. Their ingrained in history forever. I do not have regrets, because that's who I was. That's what I thought. And I cannot apologise for that. It would be unfair on myself."

The lawyer turned to the judge. "You see your honour. He shows no remorse for the murder." He looked back at Adrian. "Instead he chooses self-satisfaction. A balance that in his mind is fair." Adrian sniggered at the lawyer.

"I will now present you, my colleagues and invited members of the public with all the evidence we have gathered and tell you a harrowing story with help of course, from Mr Leones and selected witnesses."

The judge cleared his throat. "Well let's get this over with. Where do we start?"

* * *

"Proof that Adrian is a manipulative, sadistic and cold-hearted individual." The lawyer's words were unforgiving. They cut deep into Adrian's soul and whatever dignity was left was being torn to shreds.

Antony stood in the box adjacent to him, on the other side of the judge. He had recalled the angry confrontations he and Adrian had. How it all amounted to personal gain for only one person, Adrian. Adrian's emotionless expression became a theme for the whole afternoon. He showed no guilt for what he had done and no sympathy for anyone. When asked by the lawyer why he did not show any respect for his friend Adrian simply replied, "I got there first."

Then came the gruesome details of the night he finally confessed.

"The only reason you are not being tried for the murder of your own mother is because of the accounts given by the eye witnesses. Who, laughably, are themselves criminals." The lawyer smirked. "What do you know about Simon, Mr Leones?"

Adrian gave the shortest answer he could. "He was part of the gang with my father and mother."

"How did he know you?"

Adrian was exasperated. He felt like it was stupid question. "The gang must know all relations their employees have. I'm their son of course they would know me."

"Ah but there was another reason wasn't there?" The lawyer raised his eyebrows. "Tell me about Lucas?"

"Simon's boss was close friends with Lucas. Coincidently, Lucas became my mum's employer after she escaped Sinaloa Cartel. Lucas was like a mad scientist. His invention gave me this scar." Adrian showed the courtroom his scarred and uneven wrist. The audience remained silent.

"You know more about his 'inventions' then you let on don't you?" The lawyer walked over to his desk and grabbed a photo. He then turned the projector on at the side of the room which projected the same image. He showed Adrian the photo. "This is you. Two and a half years ago. Approaching the New Pittsburgh research facility, where Lucas worked. What were you doing there? What did you learn that day?"

Adrian gulped. "I was following Salazar. After they tried to rob the school I started to keep tabs on him. He led me into Luca's secret lab. I saw dead people connected with tubes. Blood was running into and out of them. It was like a scene from a horror movie."

"Why didn't you notify the police?"

"This was bigger than me. Bigger than you. I didn't want to get involved. Until they kidnapped me in New York."

"Your duty as a citizen Mr Leones would be to report this… criminal activity. Or you yourself are committing an act of crime."

"After all this surely you would understand, I knew what I was doing."

"In your own world Mr Leones. Not the one you share with everybody else. You may be special, but underneath, you're just as bad as the choices your parents made. That is why no case can be made for your freedom in this world." The lawyer turned away from Adrian and walked back to his seat. As he sat down he unbuttoned his blazer and spread it apart. The atmosphere in the courtroom was eerie. Adrian knew he had not done himself any favours. His true colours were showing and his future was bleak.

The judge finished writing some notes before addressing the courtroom. "Before I deliver the sentencing, I would like to offer Adrian an opportunity to have any last words."

The judge caught Adrian by surprise. He never believed he would have this opportunity. The judge looked at him closely.

"Well, are you gonna say something?"

"Yes." Adrian replied. He cleared his throat. "Never has anyone been given quite as much as an opportunity to do things right than I have. Yet, here I stand. The cause of my own downfall. I've made mistakes, bad decisions. I'm truly sorry for what I have done. But I know that means nothing. Why should you believe me? I have wasted my talent. My life. So did my parents with the choices they made. The world is a better place without me. That's all." Adrian looked over to Alexa whose eyes sparkled. The light reflected off the tears running down her face.

Adrian had learned to live his life through a mask. A front that he had used to prevent people from seeing the person underneath. An individual who was battling his own thoughts and fears. His own dreams and mistakes. It was a sad story. But it would always be Adrian's story.

Lost My Way

Five Years Ago. Pittsburgh always looked better in the sunset. The light orange haze shined upon the clouds above and the tall buildings below. A gentle breeze whisked its way through the maze of the town. Ella waited by the front door for Adrian to return home. He trudged up his driveway at snail's pace holding his dad's old baseball bat. Ella could only smile as he passed her into the house. He had turned out more perfect than she could have imagined.

"Where's dad?" Adrian asked as he put the bat down and poured himself a glass of water.

"He's out with his friends."

"Mmmm that smells lovely." Adrian's attention was drawn to the pot boiling above the gas cooker.

"You'll have to wait, it'll be ready in about half an hour." Ella moved over to Adrian and fluffed his hair. Adrian shook off her hand and ran upstairs to his bedroom.

Half an hour later Ella called Adrian down. He sat down adjacent to his mother and started eating straight away. Then Adrian paused and looked up at his mother.

"Why doesn't Dad join us for dinner anymore? He's always with his friends."

"He's just having fun Adrian. He worked hard to raise you and this family. He deserves to have some fun."

Adrian shrugged and did not speak again. He finished his dinner, put his plate in the sink and ran back upstairs to his room. Ella was left on her own in the kitchen. She sighed and finished her dinner.

After a few hours on his computer Adrian decided to call it a day. He pulled on his pyjamas and slid into his bed, drawing the covers over himself and resting his head on the pillow. Adrian often dreamed of becoming a champion. Whether it was on the field or receiving an accolade for a world-changing achievement. The images would fill his vision. The excitement

THE FRONT

filled his head. The crowd chanted his name. The noise soon turned to a whisper.

"Adrian. Adrian."

Adrian clasped his eyes shut. He did not want to wake up.

The voice continued to draw his attention. "Adrian. Adrian."

Curiosity got the better of him. He gently lifted open his eyes to the watchful stare of his father, Peter. He was half supported by the door and his own shaky legs. The strong smell of alcohol made its way over to Adrian as he groaned, still half-asleep.

"Dad leave me alone." Adrian muttered under his breath. His dad did not move.

"Adrian, I have… something to show you." Peter pointed out his finger to Adrian then quickly withdrew it to keep his balance. "It's very cooool." The tone of his voice got higher with each word.

"I'm trying to sleep." Adrian raised his voice. He turned his back and lifted the cover over himself.

"C'mon this'll only take… like… a second."

Adrian sighed from under the covers. He pulled down his duvet and climbed out of bed. He was only wearing his pyjama bottoms.

"Jesus do you wear clothes?" Peter started to wave around his hands in front of his eyes to shield his view. Adrian tiptoed to his wardrobe and slipped on a plain white t-shirt.

"What did you wanna show me dad?"

Peter looked up at Adrian and smiled. "Follow me." He used his head to point them out the door. As he led Adrian through the hallway he tilted left and right taking small steps to regain his balance. Adrian could only shake his head in disappointment as Peter bumped into the walls and small parts of furniture dotted along their path. Surprisingly Peter made it down the stairs unscathed.

At the bottom Peter stopped and waited for Adrian to catch up behind him.

"This way." Peter whispered.

He led Adrian across to the garage. With sobering attention Peter quietly turned the door handle clockwise and pushed firmly. The door creaked with a strangely comforting tone. Peter stumbled through, taking no notice of the darkness he was in. Adrian followed behind, flicking on the light switch to his left. He was left stunned by what he saw next. Frozen. Speechless. Concerned.

The right hand side of his dad's car was in pieces scattered across the floor. The rest of the car was pushed up against the wall, diagonal to the room. Adrian looked further at his father. He could see cuts and bruises on his face and arms made clearer by the light. Peter was completely oblivious to it all. That is what concerned Adrian the most. Peter continued to walk along a skewed path towards the back seat of the car. He pulled open the car door and circled his eyes inside. He then stepped back and stretched towards the second seat, reaching for a small object placed accurately in the centre. As the object was pulled from the door's shadow Adrian looked on in horror.

"Dad, why do you have a gun?" Adrian stepped back an inch. His dad was cradling the handgun in the palm of his hand. His finger was placed dangerously close to the trigger. Adrian could sense the impending danger. Peter looked at his son dead in his eyes.

"It's a secret Adrian."

It was like his father had instantly sobered up. Peter's posture straightened, his voice lowered and his stare continued. Adrian inched further away.

"Dad?" His soft voice questioned. "Why do you have a gun?"

"Adrian, I do not live an honest life." Peter took large steps closer to Adrian. He rubbed the back of his hand across Adrian's left cheek. "I did not mean to hurt you. You're my son and I love you. You have to remember that. But I've put your life in danger. It's time you knew the truth."

"What are you talking about?" Adrian took a small gulp, too scared to take a breath.

"I ship drugs for a living Adrian. I balance the books of a criminal organisation. I've murdered people in cold blood."

Adrian finally exhaled. His stuttering breath reflected his anxiety and shock. He whispered the simplest of questions. "Why?"

"I had to. I wasn't going anywhere." Peter started to break down in tears. His back arched forwards and he held his face with the palm of his hand. His fingers wiped the tears away from his eyes.

"And what about me?" Adrian shouted. He showed no sympathy for his father. "You never even shared a thought about me." His voice lowered again.

"Adrian... I didn't have a choice." Peter looked like a helpless man. He sat on the floor with his head still buried in his hands.

"You always have a choice Dad. You made the wrong one."

Peter shook his head in disagreement.

"Does Mum know?"

Peter lifted his head up. "You can't tell her Adrian."

"What?" Adrian was in disbelief. "You need help Dad!"

Adrian turned away to exit the garage. But before he could step foot outside he felt Peter's hand grasp his arm and pull him back with great force. His head swung around to face his father. Peter held the gun against the side of Adrian's head. Peter's sadness had turned to anger.

He gritted his teeth. "You're not going to say anything," he threatened.

Adrian started to panic. His face painted a picture of shock. He was seeing a different side to his father. He tried to escape his grip but he heard Peter roll his finger towards the trigger. Adrian felt like he had been backed into a corner. He tried to communicate with his deranged father.

"Dad you don't have to do this. Take a good look, I thought you wanted to protect me."

"I'm protecting both of us." Peter replied, his voice raised. "Now please, just get in the car."

"What?" Adrian responded. His dad backed off but kept the gun pointing directly at his chest. He gestured towards the car.

"We need to take a trip."

"Dad, I'm not going anywhere with you in this state. Let's just go back inside and talk."

"Talking will get us nowhere. Now get in the car."

Adrian hesitated. Peter's patience was running thin. He stared at Adrian with those familiar cold and dead eyes. Adrian could almost see the flames rage inside his head. He decided to make one more appeal to his father.

"Dad, this isn't you. This isn't right!"

Peter sighed. "I'm not going to hurt you Adrian." He spoke his words almost as if it was supposed to offer a level of comfort. But Adrian was still as frightened as ever. He had good reason. Contradicting his words as soon as he said them, Peter grabbed the front of his gun and thumped the side of Adrian's head with the back of his weapon. Almost instantly Adrian fell to the ground, unconscious. Peter picked up his son's unresponsive body from the floor and carried him over to the passenger seat of the crashed car.

Peter reversed the car out of the garage and into the clear night. The streets were silent. The street lights shined brightly onto the roads below. The dented car was barely noticeable as it strode smoothly along. Adrian lay in the passenger's seat with no idea where he was going, what he was going to see and what was going to happen.

Murder

Surrounded by darkness, this was not the place Adrian wanted to be. He was stuck on a chair, his hands tied up behind his back. He could feel his head pounding, the pain centralised to where Peter had knocked him out. All Adrian could do was quietly groan and tilt his head back and forth. As he awoke his heart pounded quicker. The extent of the situation was dawning on him.

Before Adrian could react he saw a light shine in the corner of the room. It was surprisingly far away. He was not in a small or even large room. He was in a warehouse. The ceiling above him was raised almost thirty feet above him. The small light seemed miles away from where he was sat. The light then started to move. It was getting closer to him. Until it was shining in his face and blinding his eyes. Adrian closed his eyes and turned his head away from it.

"Welcome back Adrian." Peter moved the torch away from Adrian's face and onto his own. Adrian turned back towards his father.

"Where am I?"

"Somewhere safe." Peter replied.

Adrian could not help but think he was lying. He was not believing anything his father told him now.

"Why am I here?"

"Adrian... I have to keep you safe. It's my job. The only way I can do that is to take you away from the world.

"Take me away from the world, Dad!" Adrian's breathing quickened. "Are you going to kill me!?"

"When people ask too many questions Adrian... I have to silence them." The tone of Peter's voice became more direct and dominant.

"You can't do this. What are you talking about?

Peter was growing tired of Adrian's whining. "You just don't stop talking do you?"

MURDER

Peter's hands appeared out of the shadows. His left hand was empty but his right hand held a long and thick roll of black sticky tape. He stretched it out in front of Adrian and tore about fifteen centimetres off. He then leant over and pushed it into Adrian's face, covering his mouth and leaving only his groans to be heard. Peter took a couple of steps back. He shined his torch onto a bag next to him. It was a small black bag with lots of pockets at the front and the side. Peter zipped down the main part of the bag in the centre. He pulled out a short but deadly pistol and passed in onto his right hand. He reached back into the bag and grabbed a long black tube. A silencer. Adrian gasped. Peter stood up straight and looked at Adrian.

"It'll be painless." His evil voice echoed across the warehouse. He attached the silencer onto the end of the pistol and began to screw it in tighter.

Adrian did not have a choice. He was staring death in the face of his father. Adrian extended out his wrists and broke the rope tied to his hands with frightening pace. He ripped the tape off his mouth and then stood directly in front of his father. Adrian was determined to show Peter that he was the bigger man and that this night was not going to end in tragedy.

Peter did not react. It was like he expected to see Adrian show an incredible amount of strength. "You think you're so special don't you?"

"I won't let you end my life." Adrian stayed defiant and unnerved by his father's reaction.

"We are cut from the same cloth you and I Adrian."

"We're not the same." Adrian challenged.

"I used to have your abilities too Adrian. It's something that just disappears with age. And when that happens, it drives you crazy inside." Peter spoke his words like a mad man.

"I don't care about this. That's what you don't understand." Adrian moved a step closer to him and knocked the pistol out of his hand. "Life isn't about looking at what you had or what you want. It's about what you have now. It's about making the most of everything you have. Strength or weakness."

Peter chuckled. "I wish I could be proud of you Adrian. But you're just as stupid as everyone else. You think you're so perfect."

It was Adrian's turn to be angry. "You're a terrible man. And it's time someone taught you that."

Adrian sent a powerful left fist soaring into Peter's cheek, sending him flying backwards across the floor. Peter turned to face the ceiling, his mouth dripping with blood. He did not have the strength to stand up. Adrian picked up the pistol and walked over to his father. He towered over his bleeding and pitiful state.

"This is who you are Adrian." Peter stated.

Adrian stood in silence, frozen.

"You're a murderer at heart." Peter continued. "Just like your father."

Adrian raised the gun and pointed it directly at Peter's chest. He pulled back the trigger twice. Two silent bullets pierced through Peter's shirt and tore a hole in his heart. Peter's body jolted upwards as he used his hands to cover his chest. He groaned in pain. Then silence. Peter's lifeless body fell to the floor. Adrian drew breath. He lowered the gun to his side and dropped it. The crash echoed across the murky room. Nothing about this made Adrian feel right. He collapsed to his knees and started to cry into the palms of his hands. His head was full of regret. The whole world came crashing down onto his shoulders.

It took a while for Adrian to stand up and think through his next steps. There was no doubt if people knew the truth he would be put on trial. But if he kept it a secret he could continue to live his life normally. At least as normal as it could be without a father and a broken mother. But it was better if she did not know anything. About the gang, about the person he really was. It was time to hide the truth. Adrian grabbed his father's left arm and dragged it across the warehouse to the door at the far end. It was a walk that seemed like miles. Adrian had to use both his hands to create any type of force against the friction of the floor. The floor was covered in dust, dirt and stones. He could hear it rattle and crumble underneath his father's dead body.

Once Adrian was outside he glanced around at his surroundings. He could see his father's car abandoned on the side. In front of him were rows of trees. The deep fog and mist prevented Adrian from seeing any further. But he knew he was in the middle of a forest. *The perfect hiding place.* He pulled his father's body towards the visible trees. As he battled through the loose branches he found a blank patch of mud. Adrian hauled his father in the centre and then dropped to his knees beside him. Using just his hands, he began to dig deep into the ground and push out the soil and leaves. Once the hole was deep enough, Adrian rolled his father into it. Peter's face planted onto the ground. As Adrian gathered the soil and dirt, the moonlight drifted through the fog and illuminated his makeshift grave. He took a moment to look at his father's body. Then he poured the mixture over Peter's head and buried him into the Earth.

Adrian pulled himself to his feet. He lifted up the hood on his black jacket and took another quick glance at his environment. There seemed to be a narrow footpath leading away from the warehouse. It was his best chance of getting home. Adrian took a deep breath. It condensed in the air. The night had gotten colder. He took his first step away from his buried father. There was no looking back now. He was focused on the path in front of him. With that thought engrained on his mind, he disappeared into the dark, cold mist.

Live Forever

Twenty-Five Years Later. Today was a special day. The day Adrian had been waiting twenty years for. The final day of his sentence. The time had come.

Adrian stared down the long corridor. The brightness of the sun lit up the far end. He could sense the freedom. Adrian dragged his feet along the wide path. His slim figure was slouched forward and his eyes were half-closed. It had been a long time since Adrian could look forward to the path stretched out in front of him. He had almost forgotten what freedom felt like.

Adrian stopped halfway down the corridor at the reception desk. A guard turned towards the window and took a long look at Adrian. The guard was dressed in light blue uniform and wore a policeman's cap with a badge stuck to the front. Three bold words spread across the bottom of the badge. Honour Integrity Service. Adrian smirked as his gaze lowered towards the guard's face.

"Where's my stuff?" Adrian asked intently.

"What stuff?" The guard sniffed at the question.

"Did you miss the training where they taught you what Integrity means?" Adrian smiled in the face of the guard.

The guard leaned forward. He stared at Adrian with a face full of thunder. He was centimetres away from the glass screen, the only thing separating him from Adrian. Then the guard backed away and reached into his desk below. He pulled out a small shoebox and dropped it on top of the desk. Adrian watched intriguingly as the guard took each item out one at a time. First a small amount of cash was placed on the counter. Adrian picked it up and counted it. He had about thirty-five dollars to live off. Next, the guard found his watch. The glass face reflected the sunlight into Adrian's eyes. He stared at it for a moment before wrapping it back onto his wrist. The time had stopped at 8:32am. Adrian wondered if a battery with lifelong charge had been invented during his time in prison. Probably not. The world he left was in decline. The final item returned to Adrian was his keys. Of course, he had no home to return to. They were useless. But he wanted to keep his key ring. It was a flat piece of red metal shaped like a diamond with four distinct edges. He placed it straight into his front trouser pocket. Adrian turned back to the guard who gestured towards the exit of the prison.

With pride, Adrian lifted his head and again faced the path outside. Each step lifted more weight off his shoulders. The light closed in. The darkness subsided. Suddenly, Adrian had a life not governed by society. He had no family. He had no friends. He had no problems. Most importantly, however, he had no life. His mind, body and soul was simply empty.

* * *

"Adrian, turn around."

Ella's soft voice greeted the silent young man. Adrian admired his mother.

"I didn't mean it." Adrian stretched out his hand. She remained unmoved. Another hand grabbed her shoulder from behind.

"Dad?"

Adrian's father moved into the picture, holding onto Ella and smiling at Adrian. He was well-dressed and looked a shadow of the man Adrian had left behind.

"I think it's time we talked." Peter said still resting his hand on Ella's shoulder. The two of them nodded.

"I'm sorry." Adrian replied.

"You've no need to be sorry Adrian." Ella tilted her head in a calming manner. "It was our fault."

Adrian was confused. "I don't understand."

"We don't blame you." Ella responded.

"Adrian, it was our mistakes. We're sorry." Peter moved to the side of Ella. "We were wrong to think you would be different."

"You still don't get it." Adrian still felt like he was being played by his parents. "I am different. And those were my mistakes."

"You wouldn't have had the chance to make those mistakes without us." Ella replied.

"The decisions that I made were not governed by you." Adrian's anger was growing. "If I knew better then…"

"Then what Adrian?" Ella wanted to hear what Adrian was going to say.

"Everybody makes mistakes. What makes others different is the way they respond." Adrian lowered his tone. "If I was a better person, if I was stronger… I wouldn't have been in the position I was."

Ella and Peter looked at each other and smiled. "That's what we wanted to hear." Peter moved closer to Adrian.

Adrian's dropped his head. "It's too late now isn't it?"

"Yes. But you are free now. We are all free." Peter held out his hand. Adrian grabbed it and gave his father a firm handshake. He could not let go. He turned to his mother and looked into her proud eyes. He spread his arms apart and wrapped them around Ella. They both shed tears. But Adrian had one last question. He turned to his father.

"Then what is the meaning of life?"

Peter smiled. "Life is what you make of it Adrian. There is no set of rules for existence. There isn't one way you can think." He put his arm around Adrian. "You are simply placed in reality and it's up to us to forge meaning and build identity."

In room 107 of Motel 6 in Pittsburgh a fallen chair lay in the middle. There was a hook attached to the ceiling, only recently installed. Wrapped over the hook was a thick rope that extended down about 4 feet. The other end of the rope enveloped a human's neck. The weight of the human body helped the rope squeeze tighter. The body lay still, resting by the hand of the rope. There was no marks of a struggle. For this person it was easy. All that was left behind was a small note placed over a diary next to him. Written inside was four words.

Forge Meaning,
Build Identity

THE END

Acknowledgments

Wow! It is done. The story's told. I hope you enjoyed reading it. This was a very different project for me to take on but I have enjoyed every moment. I would just like to share some of my thoughts about the story before I get onto acknowledging important people. Although this is just a story some of it is based on my own personal experiences that I have told through different characters and pieces of fiction. It took a lot of consideration to decide whether I would share these moments. But this is what I wanted to leave behind and it adds so much value to a novel that will always hold a special part in my heart.

I would first like to thank my closest family; my mother, father, brother and sister. They have all been so supportive through my years whether it was financially, emotionally or morally. Thank you to my mother, for letting me grow up with a free mind and one that wants to do right. Thank you Rishi, you have always been the funny one in the family and the laugh I go home for. I hope you find happiness in whatever you do. Thank you Anisha, the sister that encouraged my academic side and was always up for a philosophical conversation. Without this I would not have the mind I have now. I hope you find your place in this world because no one else deserves it more. For this part of my family, I will always be there for support whenever you need it because it is the least I can do.

Next my long-time friend Anton. Thanks for sticking by me all these years, it's been great that we've kept in touch. I will never be able to have the same conversations with anyone else about anything! I hope you do well in the future. Thirdly, the people I lived with during the best years of my life so far and the place for the majority of my editing. My housemates of three years; Fred, Rob, Harry, Jess and Alice. You have all been my rock during this process. You gave me the support when I needed it, the jokes when I was down and the will to become the person I am today. Thank you! I hope you all go on to be successful in your lives. To the people I studied my degree with; Tom, Ruby, Rachael, Nick, Dan, Wilson and the rest of the Physics class of 2015 at York! Thank you for all the help you have offered me and all the laughs we shared together. You are the people that have the minds to truly impact the world in a positive way. You are the most skilled graduates that leave University every year so make it count. Good luck to you all.

Printed in Great Britain
by Amazon.co.uk, Ltd.,
Marston Gate.